PURSUED BY THE IMPERIAL PRINCE

IMPERIAL PRINCES OF THE LATHAR

MINA CARTER

NEW YORK TIMES & USA TODAY BESTSELLING AUTHOR

Copyright © 2011 by Mina Carter

Second Edition © 2017

Third Edition © 2021

All rights reserved.

No part of this book may be reproduced in any form or by any electronic or mechanical means, including information storage and retrieval systems, without written permission from the author, except for the use of brief quotations in a book review.

PROLOGUE

"You don't have to go through with this, you know that... don't you, darling?"

Jaida smiled. "Dad, I'll be fine."

"Are you sure?"

Duke Lianl's eyes were full of concern as he turned her to face him. His hands paused for a second on her armbands, then slid down to her hands. The armbands were new, to mark her coming of age. "You're only eighteen Jaida. We can put this off a year or... ten maybe?"

"Dad, it's fine. I'm fine. I'm all grown up now. You worry too much." She chuckled, a light sound of amusement. Nothing could bother her today.

Her father smiled as he swept a look over her.

His eyes were the same color as hers, deep sapphire ringed with the silver of royal blood.

"You look just like your mother. She'd have been so proud of you—" Duke Lianl broke off as a familiar sadness filled his eyes. She'd been dead ten years, but Malden Lianl had never forgotten his wife.

"Thank you. I hope she would have," She squeezed his hands softly before letting go and then tucked her hand into the crook of his arm. "Shall we?"

"If you're sure."

Her father gave in with a small sigh, but she caught the gleam of pride in his eye as he straightened up and gave a nod to the servant at the door. They were ready. The servant pushed the doors open ahead of them, and her stomach clenched. This was it. The moment she'd been dreaming of for years.

"His grace, Lord Malden, the Duke of Lianl, and his daughter, the Lady Jaida," the herald announced. His rich voice rolled around the cavernous ballroom, a ringing voice that drew the attention of the crowds gathered below.

Would he be here? Jaida's heart clambered into her throat, trying to escape the manic butterflies racing around her stomach. Shivers chased each other over her skin as Jaida and her father neared the top of the formal staircase. Wide and sweeping, it made a grand entrance into the palace ballroom, and as tradition dictated, every debutante walked down those steps to take her place in society.

Jaida's heart stuttered to a stop, no longer beating wildly against the formal silk of her gown as everyone in the ballroom below turned to look up at them. Her knees trembled, knocking together so loudly she was surprised the people below couldn't hear them.

Unable to help herself, Jaida lifted her eyes and looked out over the ballroom below. The floor was a kaleidoscope of color. The bright silks and satins of the women's formal gowns contrasted sharply with the somber grays and greens of the men.

Her gaze swept over the hall. Had all these people really turned out just to see her presented to the court? Her eyes searched the crowds, looking for one figure. He had to be here. A tall, broad shouldered figure dressed in black and wearing the sash of royal blood. Her breath caught in her throat as her gaze collided with piercing silver.

He *was* here.

His highness, Prince Sethan Kai Renza. Not just a royal prince, but an imperial prince, and the most eligible bachelor in the Combined Systems of the Fifth Princedom. The only man she was interested in seeing.

Everything faded into the background as he moved toward her, the crowd parting like water before him.

Her hand tightened on her father's arm as they drew to a stop at the head of the stairs. They would remain there until she was formally invited to the court, then she would walk down alone. It was a journey that signified her transition from childhood to womanhood and marked her as eligible for marriage.

"Breathe, little one," her father said softly, obviously misconstruing her tension to be nerves. "Imagine them in their underwear if that helps."

"Dad!"

"Especially Kai-Renza. I remember him as a snot-nosed brat in diapers." Duke Lianl carried on, ignoring the fact that Jaida was trying to contain her mirth and failing badly. Luckily, being at the top of the expansive staircase, only her father could hear the delicate little snorts of laughter she couldn't keep in.

"You can't say things like that! It's… I don't know, treason maybe?"

The Duke shrugged, but the amusement drained from his face. Below them, the Prince stepped forward.

"What the hell… " Her father's voice echoed shock as Sethan strode to the bottom of the staircase in a total breach of protocol.

What was he doing? The tension in her father's body was catching, flowing through to Jaida.

"Duke Lianl, it's a pleasure to see you at court again." Sethan inclined his head in deference to her father's status as a royal duke. Then he turned his attention to Jaida, and heat flared in his quicksilver eyes. She shivered. It felt like her soul had been branded. Then Seth did something no one expected.

He bent into a deep bow before straightening and extending his hand to her. "My lady, would you do me the honor?"

CHAPTER 1

"Move that *draanthing* piece of shit… Yeah, I'm talking to you buddy. Sheesh, some people really need to learn to drive."

Jaida slumped back into the harness of her power loader and concentrated on transferring the load she was carrying from the open cargo hold to the anti-grav pallets. She grumbled under her breath as she worked. Today was not a good day. The idiot-factor was so high she was virtually swimming in them.

She shook her head, her dark hair dancing about her shoulders, and issued another curse directed at *draanthic* who wanted to load high and drive fast. Yeah, she was just as interested in her weekly bonus as anyone else, but there was no way she was risking a safety fine. Especially not when her rent was due.

She moved smoothly, arms and legs activating the sensor plates in the bi-pedal loader as she transferred her load container by container. A tired sigh escaped her lips as the last one slid into place with a heavy *clunk-click*. The red light on the side of the full pallet flicked to green and it moved away on automatic, a fresh one sliding into place in front of her.

"Hey *chica*, almost quittin' time... You working over today?"

Jaida turned at the voice, the feet of the loader clunking against the deck plating until she could see the voice's owner. Felis, the only other woman on the team, smiled back at her through her front screen.

Jaida rolled her shoulders to ease the ache creeping across them. "Yeah, I am. Could do with the extra cash, and you know what'll happen if the Galess shipment doesn't get offloaded in good time. Hicks'll pitch a hissy fit, and tomorrow will be down the shitter before we start."

She smothered a sigh at her language, automatically coarse to match her cover identity. She'd been everything from a high-speed courier on Arcalis Prime to a waitress in the cloud cafés on Selenis. Different careers, different names, different identities. When a cover got this complete and easy, so easy she started to believe in it herself, she knew she'd been in the same place too long.

It was time to move on, before she got comfortable and started to make mistakes. Mistakes would allow Seth to find her, and then people would die. They always did. Trouble was she liked Felis and the guys. For the first time in years, she felt at home. If a wanted woman could relax enough to feel at home anywhere.

"Jai! Boss wants to see you in the office."

Another voice interrupted their conversation. Both loaders turned at the heavy *clump-whirr-clump* of an approaching crane-lifter. Jaida hid her shudder as the driver leered at them. All the women on the docks knew about Hanrahan—they'd all been subjected to his sexist and suggestive comments.

"Hey Jai, you want a hand getting out of that tin can? Perhaps a little bit of a rubdown?"

"No thanks Han, I might catch something." She turned away in a whir of mechanics, rolling her eyes as she passed Felis. "Best see what the boss man wants. Catch you tomorrow if I'm not out before you leave."

"Okay, good luck sweets. Mood he's been in, you may need it."

* * *

"Jai's one of our best loaders… precise and fast. Keeps to herself. Never had a bit of trouble with her. Polite and easy to get along with, the others all like her… " The docking bay manager's voice trailed off as the man at the window turned and fixed him with an iron gaze.

"She's a criminal, Mr. Gregaris, not at all the sort of person you want in your employment."

Seth's voice was quiet, but inside he was seething. He turned back to the window as the loader rounded the last corner and started down the straight walkway toward the offices. He watched it approach, his face an impassive mask. He'd learned early in life never to show weakness or reveal the chinks in his armor. As chinks went, they didn't get much bigger than Lady Jaida Lianl.

He would have given her anything she ever wanted, the universe itself. But she'd chosen to run instead.

The loader clumped to a stop below him and a force field snapped into place around the bay. The blue-turquoise haze was unmistakable, shimmering as oxygen was pumped into the enclosed area. The air vents on the hatch popped, releasing the pressure in twin geysers as the canopy lifted. A small, slender figure emerged and climbed down the front of the large machine with an ease that spoke of long practice.

Seth's anger started to mount again. She would rather do manual labor than be with him? If it was work she wanted, then he'd be sure to give it to her… on her back in his bed.

"She's a criminal?" The dock manager sounded confused. "Begging your pardon, Your Highness, but are you sure you have the right woman? Jai… no, I can't believe she'd even *think* about breaking the law. She's a stickler for rules. Always lecturing the others about safety rules and everything."

Below Seth, the woman walked toward the door, pausing for a moment to look up as though she sensed what awaited her.

"Perfectly sure, Mr. Gregaris." Seth bit back the surge of triumph. There could be no mistake. It *was* her. He resisted the urge to step back. She couldn't see him up here, and even if she could, there was no way out. His men had the bay surrounded and his second in command was in place at the single room apartment she rented. There was no escape. Not for Jaida.

Not from him. Not now.

There never had been.

* * *

SOMETHING WAS WRONG. Jaida reached the main doors and paused for a moment as a tendril of dread wound its way up her spine. Narrowing her eyes she tried to get a look into the lobby ahead as she passed through the first set of sliding doors. She couldn't linger here. The bay was on a time sequence. In five minutes the force field would snap off, and she'd be left trying to breathe hard vacuum. Something she didn't particularly fancy doing.

Rock and a hard place. She stepped forward. The doors slid shut behind her with a solid *clunk*. The sound rolled through her like a death knell. Her instincts screamed at her to run, not step into the reception lobby.

"Crap, crap, crap. This is such a bad idea."

She moved forward to the doors and tried to peer through them as the airlock went through its cycle. She'd always thought it was overkill, what with the bay outside, but now she was glad of the delay. Trying for nonchalance, she scanned the lobby. Already her agile mind was working out all the routes out of the building.

Miriam, the receptionist, sat behind the large flexi-glass-and-steel desk, headset on and hands moving swiftly over the holo-console in front of her. Her fingers twisted and pinched as she worked, plucking at images Jaida couldn't see from this side of the desk.

She scanned around, her vision panning from one side of the room to the other. Opposite the reception desk, a small group of couches sat in front of full-length windows overlooking the loading docks. Having worked on them for months, Jai would have picked a different view. Even a blank wall would have been preferable.

Nothing was out of place, not even a leaf on the expensive Terranian palms in the corner.

"Okay, jumping at shadows. Get a grip, Jai," she told herself as the doors in front of her slid open and she stepped through.

"Morning Miriam, boss called me. Shall I wait?"

Jaida headed toward the chairs discreetly hidden behind the palms. Unlike the plush couches for the visitors, these were hard, wipe-clean plastic. For the workers, people like her. The dregs of society. A long time ago she'd have sat on the couches and not thought a thing about it.

Those days were long gone. She went to sit on the chair nearest to the lift door.

"No. Go on up, go right in." Miriam said.

One eyebrow winging up in surprise, Jaida stood and headed that way. It wasn't until the door slid shut behind her and the lift started up that she processed what Miriam had said.

Go right in.

No one went right into Gregaris' office. He was an approachable guy, if a bit blunt, but even so, no one went right into his office. The sense something was wrong hit her in the gut again, stealing her breath. The lift was too small. She couldn't escape. For five years she'd made sure she always had an escape route, always had a way out. Panic clawed at her gut and her heart climbed into her throat.

Something was wrong. She dragged deep breaths into her lungs and forced her heart rate back down to something approaching normal. It worked, but only just. Her heart pounded and slammed against her ribcage. The sides of her neck hurt with all the tension as she battled her fight-or-flight instincts.

Gradually she got them under control, biting her lower lip as she watched the numbers above the door count up. Sweat slid between her shoulder blades and down the valley between her breasts.

Nothing was wrong; there was no way Seth could have found her here, not with all the hoops she'd jumped through to set up this identity. A lot of money had changed hands for her to get the ID and med numbers of a kid who'd died at seven but whose parents had never registered the death. Med numbers were worth their weight in gold.

The door pinged. She gulped a lungful of air as they slid open to reveal the corridor beyond. It was empty.

Shaking her head Jaida stepped out the lift and walked toward Gregaris' office. Plush carpeting under her feet ate the sound of her steps as she approached the door. Her hand reached out, was almost at the handle, when she paused. A frown creased her brow.

Something *was* wrong. The instincts that had been clamoring since the lobby ganged up on her and became tribal screaming. This time, she listened.

She snatched her hand back from the handle and turned on her heel. The space between her shoulders itched as she headed back the way she'd come. She could feel the crosshairs painted on her back, a little red mark dancing across her skin like a butterfly.

Walking past the lift door, she headed for the emergency stairs at the end of the corridor. She'd barely covered half the distance when it began to open. Her heart stilled, fluttering deep inside her chest as she started to backpedal. She knew what she'd see before the heavily armed trooper stepped through the open door.

Time slowed to a crawl as the muzzle of the trooper's rifle swung toward her. The red dot of the laser sight raced across the pale walls, then across her field of vision, blinding her for a second. She turned and raced for the lift, yelling and slamming her hands against the flat metal of the closed doors.

"No. Oh please, Lady, no…"

They'd called it back down. She jabbed at the buttons frantically as more troopers piled into the hallway. There was no way out, just the lift and the stairs currently filled by imperial guards. Or… the office at the end of the corridor, the door looming in her peripheral vision like some harbinger of doom.

"Trall…"

She abandoned the lift and raced up the corridor, grabbing at each handle as she passed, hoping beyond hope one would give. If she could just get into one of the offices, she could find a ventilation shaft or something. It wouldn't be the first time she'd escaped that way.

"Lady Jaida Lianl, by order of his Imperial Majesty, you are under arrest—"

"Screw his Imperial Majesty!"

Her hand closed around the last door handle, and wonder of wonders, it opened. She stumbled through and slammed hard into a solid chest. Strong arms closed around her. With a gasp she looked up into hard silver eyes.

Familiar silver eyes.

"I thought you'd never ask."

"No… " Her gasp of denial was automatic as she fought against his hold, vicious as a wildcat, bucking and heaving in his embrace.

"Yes." He quelled her struggles by yanking her up hard against him.

Panic and awareness flared through her at the familiar feel of his body against hers. His Imperial Highness, Prince Sethan Kai Renza. Seth. The man she'd once loved with all her heart and soul.

Defeat wrapped around her heart in a crushing embrace as she looked up. He had the face of a dark angel, all hard, masculine lines. His eyes were mercurial silver, their cast almost feline, surrounded by thick, dark lashes. A straight nose sat above sinfully full lips reputed to make even a priestess think wanton thoughts. He was as handsome as she remembered, but where his expression had once been charming, it was now hard and triumphant.

"Let me go!" She shoved at the brick wall of his chest, but it was a futile gesture. Seth was solidly built with a warrior's physique. Once it had thrilled her, but right now she'd give everything she owned to be on the other side of the galaxy.

"Anyone would think you're not pleased to see me." His drawl was rich and mellow, just a hint of his court accent tainting the galaxy-standard he spoke.

Jaida's lip curled into a sneer. "You don't think? *Goddess*, you musta been at the back of the queue when she was handing out the brains."

He winced at her words. She knew he would. The rough dock dialect would grate on his nerves just as much as the insult.

"Don't talk like that." His hand slid into the hair at her nape, and his thumb stroked along the sensitive skin at the side of her neck. Refusing to be cowed, either by his touch or his larger, more powerful body, she pulled against his hold.

"Or you'll what? Declare me an outlaw, exile me from my family, and denounce me as a criminal? Oh… wait. You already did that."

Anger flared in his silver eyes. He leaned in until

his lips brushed against her ear and whispered. "You're mine, you always were."

She snorted, an inelegant sound of amusement and contempt. "I'll never be yours, Seth. Never. Why do you think I left? You're not man enough for me."

It was a foolhardy thing to say to an Imperial prince, especially Seth, but she wasn't thinking. She wanted to hurt him. Deal a blow to his masculine pride. Her heart ached at the lie, but now that he'd caught her, it was the only weapon she had. Her heart had been shattered beyond repair anyway, so what was one more hurt?

All that mattered now was hiding the effect that seeing him again was having on her. She kept her expression cold and furious, but deep inside blood surged through her veins at his touch. The solid strength of his body against hers starting a fire low down in her belly that burned brighter every second.

"Not man enough?" His eyebrow winged up, a raven arch against his pale skin. Court pale. None of the nobility would be uncouth enough to allow their skin to tan. Well, unless they'd been on the run for five years like she had, taking any job they could just to eat and provide a roof over their head. The first thing she'd done to fit in was get a suntan.

"*Never*."

As soon as the word was out of her mouth, she knew she'd pushed too far. Fury blazed in his eyes, scorching her to her soul. His fingers tightened in her hair. She tried to turn her face away, but he hooked a finger under her chin and tugged. Not gentle, not rough, just unstoppable.

Held fast, she watched as Seth's lips descended, covered hers. A whimper escaped as he pried her lips apart and thrust his tongue past them to claim the sweetness within. The touch of his mouth shattered her defenses. Disbelief and need surged through her in equal amounts. She'd promised herself that, should the worst happen and he captured her again, she would be as cold as the grave. Wouldn't respond to him at all. To her, Sethan Kai Renza had ceased to exist as a man.

Yeah, right.

His kiss was designed to punish and humiliate, but as soon as he touched her, her body responded. The blood in her veins heated, and her breasts tightened as he held her. Her heart rate skittered and went through the roof as she developed trouble taking her next breath. Worst of all was the heat spreading out from her core. Shame burned bright banners across her cheeks.

She moaned against his lips as his tongue thrust

again, sliding along hers and demanding her response. A response she gave, tentatively at first but then with unwilling passion. Her tongue tangled with his in an erotic dance, but her heart ached. After all he'd done, how could she crave his touch?

He lifted his head. Heat and smug satisfaction colored his eyes. "Not man enough, was it?" he taunted as he stepped away.

She clamped down on the sense of loss. There was no way she wanted him touching her, not ever again.

"Take her to my room at the Babylon, and for heaven's sake, scrub the stink of the dock off her."

CHAPTER 2

*I*t was over. Her life was over.

Jaida stood by the huge picture window of the hotel's penthouse suite and looked out. Below her the city of Severnas Three lay sprawled out like a glittering jewel against the turquoise backdrop of the ocean. Severnas never slept; the city was famous for it. The pleasure capital of the galaxy. At one time, when she'd been Lady Jaida Anais Lianl, youngest daughter of the house of Lianl, she'd have reveled in its gaiety.

But she wasn't Lady Lianl anymore; she had no right to the name. She looked down at her rough, callused hands. She hadn't been a lady for a long time. Now she was just a dockworker with a bounty on her head.

She'd been here an hour already, thrown through the door by Seth's guards and told to "prepare herself." At least they hadn't taken it upon themselves to make sure she was presentable for the prince, but then she was the prince's whore. She always had been. No man would mess with something that belonged to an imperial prince.

She'd stripped out of her work coverall and bathed, luxuriating in the sumptuous bathroom suite. The guards hadn't left her anything to wear, so unwilling to put on her filthy overalls, she'd tried the replication unit. To her surprise she'd been able to access her old credit line. She'd been sure her access had been blocked years ago.

She studied her reflection. It was the same as she was used to yet not her at all. Her slender fingers reached out to stroke the cool glass. The dull, flat dye she'd used on her hair was gone and it's true, purple hues were once again revealed. The contacts that turned her eyes worker-brown were gone as well, leaving them bright in the dim light of the suite. The Lianl eyes, sapphire blue ringed with silver. Distinctive on any planet in the galaxy.

She screwed her eyelids tight as memory assaulted her. She'd been eighteen, new at court, and so innocent she hadn't seen the trap that had been set for her until it was too late.

Sethan was the handsome prince. The man of every young girl's dreams, particularly one who had grown up on the fringe of the court, desperate to be old enough to join its glittering array. Her moment in the spotlight couldn't arrive fast enough for the young girl she had been. Clad in the red of a debutante, she'd stood at the top of the stairs to the prince's court and waited for her name to be announced.

He'd been there at the bottom of the staircase, silver eyes warm with appreciation. She'd barely set foot on the top step before she was stepping from the last, her silken skirts rustling around her as she dropped into the lowest curtsy she'd ever given.

Eyes still closed; Jaida took a shuddering breath. If she'd known then what she knew now, she'd have run from that hall as fast as she could. There was no escape from Sethan. She knew that now. He was the consummate warrior-prince, famous for his ruthlessness on the battlefield and his passion in the bedroom. They said he never lost a fight he picked or a woman he chose.

Except one. One woman had run, her heart

mangled beyond repair, and she'd been branded a criminal for it.

She drew a shuddering breath and swiped at her eyes with the back of her hand. She would not cry. She wouldn't give Seth the satisfaction. She would never give him—the man who in one glorious night and one equally horrific morning had ruined her life—the satisfaction of seeing her cry.

Not then, not now, not ever.

She opened her eyes. It was time. For five years she'd put off her fate, and she was exhausted. She couldn't do it anymore. She was done running, and now she had to pay the price for trying to escape. Exhausted, she leaned against the window, her finger tips brushing the glass as her heart ached for the freedom outside the gilded cage of the luxurious room. But it was no good. Her wings were clipped and it was over.

There was nowhere left to run.

Seth stood in the corridor and tried to compose himself. She was in there. He could feel her psychic signature as it uncoiled and brushed against his mind. The delicate contact, the one he'd sought for so many years, had him hard and aching in a heartbeat.

He sucked in a harsh breath. He thought time had exaggerated his reaction to her, but the need hit him with the force of a star cruiser, as sharp and immediate as he remembered it. It had been all he could do to control himself when she'd been in his arms earlier.

She'd shielded herself. Had concealed the glory of her aura from him so he couldn't feel it. It was probably automatic. She'd spent so long hiding among commoners without a jot of psychic ability. If she hadn't learned to conceal herself, then she would have stood out like a sore thumb. Easy pickings for those he'd sent after her.

Here, where she couldn't see him and she had no need to conceal her abilities anymore, she'd relaxed a little. It was just a fraction, but it was enough to test him. He leaned his head against the cool metal of the door and sighed as he basked in her warmth. All he wanted to do was break the *draathing* door down and get in there. Gather her into his arms and claim her as his again.

He stepped through the door and paused, all his senses on alert.

His men had checked out the entire hotel, and

the sensor sweeps had confirmed it was clear, but there was no sense tempting fate. So many assassins had been sent after Seth that he'd learned never to relax his guard. The instant he did, the prick of a knife against his throat would end his life.

His gaze swept the main room of the suite. When his eyes and instincts had assured him there was nothing out of the ordinary, he looked at the petite, slender woman framed by the window. His heart slammed into his chest as triumph surged through him. At last, after so many years, he finally had her.

But it was a bittersweet victory. He had her prisoner, but unless he kept her shackled, she would be gone again.

Her back was to him, but the tension in her frame told him she knew he was there. He walked forward, his eyes caressing the lines of her figure. The purple-black hair he remembered cascaded down her back in silken waves, brushing against the creamy skin he'd spent night after night fantasizing about. The court gown bared her delicate shoulders and the sensuous curve of her spine, but the slender arms at her side were unadorned by a noblewoman's arm cuffs.

The slight plumpness of youth had faded from her cheeks and limbs, leaving a haunting air to her features and a delicacy to her build that bypassed his anger and plugged straight into his primal male instincts.

He stopped behind her, so close he could reach out and touch her. He didn't. He'd waited so long for this moment, played it out in his mind many, many times, but now that it was here, he didn't move. He'd planned to humiliate her, to take what he wanted in the most brutal way possible, then cast her aside when he got bored. Hurt her as she'd hurt him.

She stiffened, just a small movement, but Seth caught it. Her head turned to the side, just enough for him to catch a glimpse of her profile.

"How did you find me?"

Her voice was melodious and soft, betraying no emotion. Mentally he applauded her. She projected the image of the perfectly brought up lady. Even if he'd stormed in here, bloodstained blade in hand after cutting a swathe through the entire staff of the hotel, he doubted she'd do more than raise a delicately arched brow.

It was perfection, and at the same time, a total sham. Sethan gritted his teeth. He knew under that prim and proper manner there was fire and passion. Just one night with her had bewitched him.

"You've been sloppy these past couple of

months, *Jai*," he replied. She'd been working as a menial, lowly worker cleaning up after other people rather than come to him. Anger mounted.

"There was a sighting last month at the spaceport on Terranis, so I was in system when your ID was picked up here."

Jaida nodded, turning to look out the window again.

Seth's temper went up another notch. "You didn't really think you could outrun me for much longer, did you? Even if you hadn't come here… I would still have found you."

He grabbed her shoulders and spun her around to face him. His breath caught in his throat as he looked down into her face, clear of grime for the first time. Lady, she was more beautiful than he remembered. She looked up. For a split-second Seth fell into the sapphire depths of her eyes before her lids swept down. Under his hands, a tremble ran through her frame. She was scared, more than she was letting on.

Seth's lips compressed a little. Good. She should be. He leaned in, his breath stirring the curls by her ear.

"There's no escape from me, Jaida, not for you. Not ever."

. . .

SHE TRIED to stifle the shiver that ran through her body at the callused grip on her shoulders. The threat in Sethan's voice was absolute, the look in his eyes hard. He was exactly as she remembered him.

She'd once reveled in thoughts of her handsome prince and built teenage fantasies about him. Those thoughts were one she'd spent five years trying to forget. She avoided his gaze, keeping hers downcast.

"Look at me." His voice was soft, but the words were an order. The words of a man who was used to being obeyed. "Answer me. *Admit* there's no escape."

Her throat tightened. Her gaze travelled up the heavily embroidered tunic, past the open collar, and up to his jaw. Strong and shadowed with stubble, it was as far as she dared look. She wasn't a noblewoman anymore, and despite her bravery earlier, no commoner looked upon royalty directly.

"No, Your Highness, there's no escape. There never was," she replied dully, trying to deflect the storm she knew was coming.

She started to look down again, but his hand moved, driving into the hair at the nape of her neck. His fingers twined in the long strands and pulled her head back. She didn't fight; there was no point. He was stronger than she was. She kept her eyes down, refusing to look at him.

"Look at me. I won't ask again," Sethan said in a low voice. "You don't want to anger me or—"

Her gaze snapped up, and she glared at him. "Or you'll what? Hunt me across the galaxy again? This time do me a favor and kill me, okay?"

His eyes hardened but she refused to show fear. Seth's temper was as famous at court as his charm. Five years ago she'd been treated to that charm, but now, after she'd wounded his ego, she suspected she was going to get treated to the other.

"Oh no, my lady, I have something far more… pleasurable in mind than killing you." He leaned in, his intent unmistakable. She waited until his breath whispered over her lips, until his lips were mere millimeters away from hers, then she yanked her head to the side and his kiss landed on her cheek.

Seth froze. A moment later he pulled away, his warm breath fanning against her hair.

"If that's how you want it… we can play hardball. But I guarantee you won't like it."

Jaida knew better than to look up. She was sassy, yes. The places she'd been, she'd had to run her mouth off to avoid being overruled and lost in the masses. Even so, she'd never faced down any loud-mouth in a bar who was half as dangerous as Seth.

His grip tightened further on the back of her neck, forcing her to look around. She didn't want to. She tensed her neck to fight him, but it made no difference. Within seconds their standoff was over and he dragged her chin around and up. Her gaze darted to his for a second. His eyes blazed with anger, desire, and hidden beneath, a deep, dark need that frightened the life out of her.

Unable to look him in the eye a moment longer, she looked down. An answering desire flared through her body like a flash fire, leaving a simmering heat in its wake. Desperation and denial chased each other through her head.

She didn't feel anything for him, didn't *want* to feel anything for him. Not with how he'd treated her in the past… how he continued to treat her now. Like something he owned, a possession.

His arms tightened around her as he bent his head. He was going to kiss her… She stilled in anticipation and hated herself as she realized what she was doing.

Tension wound itself around the arousal that hummed through her body as she waited for her lips to be assaulted again. Deep inside, she cried for the gentle kisses he'd courted her with five years ago.

Naive as she'd been back then she'd still sensed the baser desires he'd held in check. Then, it had thrilled her. The fact that he wanted her so much, yet treated her with such reverence and care, made her feel like a princess. *His* princess.

Now though, hard reality had taught her the truth. All that had stopped when he'd gotten her into bed and taken what he wanted. Her prince charming had disappeared with her virginity, and then he'd shown his true colors.

Anger swirled around him like a cloak of darkness, but his kiss was surprisingly gentle. Firm lips slanted over hers, paused, and then moved into a slow but thorough exploration. She held herself still as he pressed feather-light kisses across her lips. One side to the other and then back again. When he'd done a complete circuit, he pulled away a little, nuzzling her nose in a gentle gesture. A gesture that could almost be mistaken for loving.

Oh, he was good. Even though she knew it was a lie, her heart threatened to melt.

"Resist me all you like." His voice was a low whisper. He had a voice that was pure temptation, husky tones that made her think of hot, sweaty nights of pleasure between cool sheets.

"I'll get what I want. I always do."

"What do you want?" she whispered helplessly against his lips. After his earlier cruelty, his gentle manner confused her. But she knew better than to believe this was the real Seth. He wanted something from her, she just didn't know what it was yet.

"I want you."

He nibbled at her lower lip and her control started to crack. Sparks of desire shot through her body, bouncing and ricocheting off each other. She shivered, wound so tightly that every sensation was increased a hundred-fold.

"I want you, all of you. I want you in my bed, your…" Seth paused to smooth his tongue over the tiny hurts he'd inflicted. "… admission that you belong to me."

Her hopes crashed and burned like a solar racer in an accident, shriveling to ash in her chest. She, this, was just vindication for him. She'd run from him and his male pride just wouldn't allow that.

"No more talking. Right now, I want to taste you. All of you."

Still numb with shock at the path her thoughts had been following, she didn't realize at first what he meant. Hooking his fingers into her gown, he started to slide the fabric off her shoulders. A quick tug and the hidden fasteners gave. The dress slid down her arms, the neckline following suit.

Jaida gasped and clutched at the falling fabric, catching it between her arms and her body. Cool air whispered over the exposed tops of her breasts. Under the silk, her nipples tightened to aching pebbles as his hungry gaze roved over her skin.

A wave of heat washed down her spine as he pulled her back into his embrace. One hard arm curled around her waist, and she leaned back, away from him.

"Nothing doing. I gave up tasting for New Year."

Even to herself her denial lacked conviction. She felt his lips quirk as he nuzzled her neck. "Want to try that again and mean it, babe?"

"Wanna *draanth* off and die?"

He didn't answer, just chuckled in amusement as a large hand spread out over the back of her hips, pulling them snugly against his. The hardness of his cock pressed against her. A spiral of arousal seared through her core as unbidden memories of their single night together assaulted her.

"Is that supposed to impress me?" she challenged, despite the fact her body clenched at the thought of him inside her. A thought that tapped into every feminine instinct she had and demanded she press against him. Insisted she rub her soft curves against the harder plains of his body in a deliberate attempt to tease him and make him follow up on the hard promise pressed against her.

She didn't. Exercising a control she had no idea she was capable of, she curled her lip. "Adequate. I guess. I've had better."

The temperature in the room dropped several degrees. Behind them there was a knock on the door. "Your Majesty? The flyer's here and waiting for you to board with your… companion."

Seth lifted his head. His eyes were as hard as diamond when he stepped away and straightened his jacket.

"Adequate? Oh, my lady, you're going to regret that," he promised, and Jaida felt the truth of his words right down to her soul. "Cover yourself, we're leaving."

CHAPTER 3

"Glorious, just glorious. She takes after her great-aunt, you know. She was Kevat's consort before your grandfather beat him in challenge."

Seth and his archchancellor stood in front of a large pane of one-way glass looking into the harem preparation chambers beyond, the man prattling away. Behind them Seth's manservant was busying himself at the refreshments table.

Seth frowned, casting a quick glance over his shoulder as Warin set a water jug down heavily on the table, the crystal crashing against the highly polished surface. Something had obviously annoyed the man. He wasn't usually so sharp with his movements. Most of the time Seth didn't know he was there. Just as a servant should be.

"They said she was like the *Kiare* flower—delicately beautiful and utterly addictive. Your grandfather risked everything, even his marriage to your grandmother, to possess her."

Seth nodded in reply, his arms folded over his chest as he watched through the window. On the other side, Jaida was surrounded by a flock of women, the robed servants fussing around her as they prepared her for his bed.

His cock hardened. Already he could see her spread across the black silk, all pale skin and dark-purple hair as she'd been that morning five years ago. Leaving her, with her lips still swollen from his kisses and the invitation in her eyes, to attend yet another council meeting had been the hardest thing he'd ever done. But, mindful of his duty and secure in the knowledge of their future together, he'd gone. As soon as the door had shut behind him, she'd fled.

Jaida was his Kiare flower.

Seth watched as the women stripped the robe from her body to leave her clad in the scarlet shift of a courtesan. A simple rectangle of cloth, it was folded and knotted around her slender curves, the traditional knot at her shoulder the key to the whole complex arrangement. Just one tug in the right place and she would be naked before him.

He shook himself out of his daze and refocused his attention on her as the women moved through their preparations. Her hip-length hair was brushed until it shone, and she'd already bathed, something Sethan had declined to watch even though he had a right to. He didn't want to see her naked just yet… No, that was a lie. If he saw her naked, it was game over. He wouldn't be able to control himself.

How he had held onto control during that little altercation in the hotel, he had no idea. He'd been giving serious consideration to handcuffing himself to the command chair on the bridge until the call came to inform him that Jaida was finished in the bathing rooms. With a last sweep of the brush through her hair and a spray of scent at her throat, the servants left her, and another woman entered the room.

"What happened to the great aunt? Jaida's?" Seth's attention was on his little kiare flower as she was inspected by the Mistress of the Harem, Keliana. His father's lead courtesan, she had retired to the honor of her own bed on his father's death and now oversaw Sethan's own harem.

"Huh?" The archchancellor blinked at Seth's

sudden question. "Oh… your grandfather made her his courtesan. She died a year later in childbirth. The only woman to ever give him a son… your uncle. Your grandfather never got over it. He forbade anyone to ever speak her name again and died less than a year after she did. Some said it was because he couldn't let her go, even in death."

Seth watched as the woman inspected Jaida's appearance. Bare toes peeked from under the silken hem as she stood motionless, her eyes fixed on the wall as she waited to be approved by the harem-mistress.

His breath caught in his throat. If Keliana didn't approve, then Jaida would be returned to the harem for further instruction before being brought to his bed. Seth's knuckles whitened. Jaida didn't need any instruction other than his, but protocol was protocol.

Finally, after walking around the younger woman three times and saying nothing, Keliana nodded. As she did, she looked at the mirrored glass, her eyes full of amusement. The harem-mistress knew he was there, watching.

It shouldn't have been a surprise. How he felt about Jaida was no secret. He'd pursued her across the galaxy for years, tracked her from planet to planet even when his advisors had told him to let it go, told him that after so long she had to be dead. But Seth couldn't let it go, wouldn't believe she was gone. Something deep down inside had told him she was still alive, the same something that wouldn't let him rest until he had her in his bed again.

His jaw set and he cut across the archchancellor's words without hearing what the man was saying. "Whatever it is, I'll take care of it in the morning. Convene the council for a noontime meeting. Until then I have some… unfinished business to take care of."

* * *

THE ROYAL SUITE WAS EMPTY.

Jaida shivered as the doors closed with a heavy clunk behind her. Blast-proof steel and flexi-glass locked her in and cut off any hope of escape. Her bare feet padded soundlessly on the plush carpeting until she was standing in the center of the huge main room. Looking around, she felt lost, bereft of purpose.

The last five years had been about avoiding Seth and his agents, about staying as far away from anything from her old life as possible. It had cost her everything. A shudder ran from the top of her head to the tips of her toes. She crammed the thoughts back into the locked room in her mind they'd escaped from and concentrated on the here and now. It was a trick she'd learned quickly, barely eighteen and on her own in the galaxy with a bounty on her head. The pampered little rich girl she'd been had disappeared within a week, replaced with someone far harder and stronger.

She would survive this. Like she had everything else. She just had to take it one step at a time.

Filling her lungs with a deep, shuddering breath she started to explore, flitting from room to room like a wraith. The sheer luxury of the place astounded her. Her family was wealthy, and as a child she'd had the best of everything. But this... her eyes widened as she stood in front of the huge bed in the master bedroom and took in the sheer opulence. This was beyond luxury.

"Reconciling yourself to your fate?" a voice asked behind her, the tone mocking. She whirled around, the silk of her gown whispering around her legs.

Seth leaned in the doorway. He watched her with a hard gaze. She hadn't heard the door open or his steps as he approached. The heavily embroidered regalia of his rank was gone, and he was dressed like the commandos she'd seen as they brought her aboard.

Like them, he wore the unrelieved black of Sector Seven, only the two lines of silver piping at his collar indicating his royal blood. On his wrist was the stylized skull tattoo of the regiment, and as if she needed further evidence of his standing, his long hair was caught into a warrior's braid.

She suppressed a shiver and backed up against the flowing drapes around the bedpost, a movement she regretted when Seth's lips quirked.

"Still running Jaida? What did I tell you about that?" He pushed off from the door frame and walked toward her. "It's not going to work. It's never going to work."

His steps were slow but deliberate as he stalked her, penning her in as she backed up around the bed. She tried to skirt around it, but there was nowhere to go. The bed was set against the wall between floor-to-ceiling windows that looked out onto the stars themselves.

Gathering her courage, she stopped and lifted her chin in defiance. "You don't scare me."

Hopefully he wouldn't notice the tremors that racked her body. It wasn't a lie; she wasn't scared of Seth. Not really. She was more scared of her reaction, her lack of control where he was concerned. Her heart hammered in her chest in a rapid tattoo, urging her to run, to get away. Instead, she stood her ground.

He leaned down, the heat of his body beating through the thin silk of her gown. She flinched and her pulse fluttered like a trapped bird in her throat.

"Then you're foolish, my lady. The things I want from you, the things I want to do to you… You should be scared."

His hands closed around her neck. Fear and excitement slammed into her gut and she lifted her hands to try and break his grip. There was a metallic *click* and he dropped his hands.

"Finally, you're mine."

Jaida's fingers shot to her throat, tracing the ornate collar he'd clipped there. Realization settled like a lead weight in her stomach.

It was a slave collar.

The band around her heart tightened.

"You can put a collar on me," she whispered. "You can put any mark of ownership on me you like, *my lord*, but I will never be yours. *Ever.*"

"Oh, I beg to differ. You're mine to do with as I wish."

He lowered his head to claim her lips. She tried to twist away, but he was too quick. His fingers tightened on the slender column of her neck. His free arm slung around the back of her waist possessively as his mouth crashed down onto hers. Prying her lips apart, he held her still as he plundered the soft recesses of her mouth. A caress designed not to please but to punish.

Fighting didn't work, but she pummeled his chest and arms anyway. His hold on her didn't lessen, just became tighter, his kiss deeper.

Desperate, she tried to shore up her defenses. This couldn't be happening. For five years she'd told herself that he was the enemy, that she hated him for what he'd taken away from her. Now she was back in his arms and his lips were on hers it was getting harder and harder to remember why she'd been running. Her resistance started to crumble as her blows stopped, her hands feathering uselessly against his shoulders.

Seth's kiss turned seductive—an assault on her senses as he cradled her head in his palms to drink from her lips. He sipped and nibbled at her mouth as though she were the finest banquet and he a starving man. With each touch he tempted her further, eroded more of the wall she'd built around her heart.

Through it all he made no attempt to touch her anywhere else, just her lips.

He didn't need to. The battlefield was Jaida's mind and crude pawing of her body would not further his campaign. From fighting his kisses, she started to anticipate them, went from avoiding the dalliance of his tongue to welcoming it.

With a whimper, the last of her defenses crumpled into dust. She kissed him back, winding her arms around his neck to press against his body until they were joined from breast to thigh.

"Mine," Seth growled, breaking away from her only long enough to sweep her into his arms. His eyes were molten silver. "Always mine."

She shivered. The tremor that ran through her body settling into her stomach to erupt into a mass of rioting butterflies. He planted a knee on the bed and lowered her into the center before he stretched out alongside her.

"I've scoured planets—whole systems—looking for you. Waiting for the next little bit of information that would lead me to where you might be, or where you'd gone next." Seth's voice was rough with passion. Or lust. Her brain was too addled to tell the difference.

"Now you're mine." His expression was serious as

he studied her. Reaching up, he brushed a strand of her hair back from her face. "I've wanted this so much for so long; I don't know where to start."

His smile and gentle admission blew her away, and her heart contracted painfully at glimpse of the charming prince he'd been. For an instant she wanted with all her heart to turn the clock back five years and start over again.

Then what? She let him charm her all over again, and in the morning he offered her a whore's silks rather than a betrothal band?

Her heart iced over.

"I believe you start with the knot." Her voice was cool and professional. Her hand hovered over the knot, her eyebrow arching as she looked up at him.

"Unless you'd like me to, my lord?"

Braced over her with his weight on his forearm Seth's eyes hardened. His jaw set, and a small muscle at the side pulsed.

"If that's the way you want it, *my lady*. I prefer my companions silent." His voice was cold as his fingers dealt with the knot at her shoulder and slowly started to un-wrap the silk from her body.

"You've changed." His voice was remote as he ran a hand down her curves, pausing at her nipple to tweak it between his fingers.

She flinched, a flush building along her cheekbones. "Well, let me call the harem mistress and get you someone who suits your lordship's *exacting* standards." Her voice was sharp as she tried to roll away.

His hands closed on her shoulders and threw her back down onto the bed.

"Oh no you don't." His voice was low and deadly. "You don't get away that easily my lady. I've spent too long getting you into my bed for that to happen. I *am* going to have you. Tonight."

Seth watched as defiance filled her eyes, and he braced himself for retaliation. He knew she was capable of it, more than capable. So many times his men had come close to capturing her, but she'd always managed to slip away. This time, though, she closed her eyes, her body limp against the sheets.

"As you wish, my lord."

Whatever Seth had expected, the stock answer of a courtesan wasn't it. Unable to hide his surprise, he looked down at her. Perhaps this was it; perhaps she'd bowed to the inevitable… After all why shouldn't she? Any sane woman faced with her situation would. He held all the cards.

When she'd run he'd been out of his mind with

worry. Where was she? Was she safe? Anger had kicked in when Warin had told him of her temper tantrum over the betrothal bracelet he'd left. The poor man had tried to conceal it from him, saying she'd left without a word but under questioning, he'd cracked and admitted that Jaida had flown into a rage because the bracelet wasn't ornate or expensive enough for her.

Furious, Seth had exiled her. Made her an outlaw and put a price on her head—one dependent on her being brought to him alive and untouched. It was the only way he could think of to protect her. Such a bounty would ensure she wouldn't fall prey to the slavers or prostitution rings in the darker reaches of the galaxy.

She had nowhere to go, nowhere to run but his bed. Any sane woman would capitulate, do the sensible thing, and agree to his terms. He was known to be generous—more than generous—to his mistresses, so she could do far worse.

Perhaps she had finally realized that? He looked down at her, lying pliant and silent in his arms with her eyes respectfully lowered. Instead of the sense of triumph he'd expected, a sense of loss filled him.

He liked her defiance. It was, always had been, a part of her charm. Even as a young girl at her debutante ball she'd challenged him, calling him out on his political viewpoints and military knowledge until a stern look from her father had silenced her. Seth had liked it, though. She was refreshing and different from all the other young girls vying for his attention.

Leaning down he whispered a kiss against her lips. Taking his time, he relearned their shape and feel. Their taste. His body, denied for so long, urged him on, urged him to part her creamy thighs and drive his cock into the slick heat of her body.

Seth braced himself above her and parted her thighs with his knee. Hands shaking with impatience, he ripped open his breeches and leaned down to kiss her throat…

She wasn't moving.

He stopped and looked down. She was motionless. If he couldn't see the rise and fall of her chest he'd swear she was one of the life-size dolls his aunt insisted on keeping in her gardens. That's what she was, a perfect china doll and just as responsive.

Seth swore, venting all his rage and frustration into a curse so foul it would make a commando blush. "This is how you're going to get your revenge, isn't it?"

He slammed his hand into the pillow by her head.

She flinched, but Seth's anger was too deep to feel sympathy. "You're going to pretend to feel nothing as I make love to you, aren't you?"

Her eyelids fluttered open and the look in her eyes speared him to the core. Once they had been filled with laughter and vitality, bright with curiosity. Now there was no laughter, just sorrow and resignation.

"This isn't love. No man loves his courtesan, he just screws her."

CHAPTER 4

Seth's eyes blazed with renewed anger and his jaw worked as though he was figuring out a reply. She had him dead to rights. Most of the nobility had courtesans; it was considered an honorable profession for the lower classes. But love? Love rarely, if ever, entered into the equation.

From the fury in his eyes, Seth didn't like being reminded of that fact. Confusion reigned in her heart. He'd started this on the morning she'd run, offering her a whore's silks instead of the betrothal band she had expected... hell, that she'd had *every right* to expect. Jaida wasn't lower class; her blood was as noble as his. For him to take her to bed, to take her virginity, and then *not* to offer marriage was an insult of the highest order.

How could he have offered her marriage though? His valet had taken great pleasure in informing her Seth was already betrothed, or as good as. The arrangements for his marriage to Princess Amelia of the sixth princedom were already underway, started long before he started to woo Jaida. Something he had completely failed to mention to her.

Their eyes stayed locked. She refused to look away. She was right, and he knew it. None of the rules of polite society or the rules that governed courtesans applied here. He'd blown that rule book out of the sky five years ago.

He opened his mouth to speak, but whatever he had been going to say was cut off by an insistent jingle from the main room. An incoming call, and if the three chirps repeated over and over again were any indication, an important one.

"I don't *draanthing* believe this," he growled and pushed off from her. Shivering at the loss of his body heat, she pulled the silk that had been her gown back around her and lay still.

Hot tears prickled at the back of her eyes, but she ignored them. She'd thought she could do this, divorce herself from her emotions and let him have what he wanted... let him screw her, spend his lust on her body until he tired of her. Then she could fade into the background, disappear to some backwater planet and live out her life without being chased. Maybe even one day find a man and have a family…

She closed down on the thought before it fully materialized. Plans like that weren't going to work, because she couldn't do this. She'd thought she could, but she couldn't. As a child she'd dreamed of what her life would be like. A child's dream of a perfect life complete with a romantic prince and a fairy-tale wedding.

Her dreams had been shattered along with her heart, but there was one thing left she couldn't shake. She couldn't just have sex with Seth, with any man she didn't love. It was a line she'd never crossed, no matter how desperate she'd been, even though the life of a whore would have provided her with enough money for a comfortable existence.

She bit her lip. If she slept with Seth then that was it. All the feelings buried deep, locked down in that part of her heart she'd sealed off five years ago, would be ripped out and exposed to the light. She didn't know if she could survive that again…

Seth's voice rumbled in the next room, carefully lowered so she couldn't pick up what he was saying. Jaida didn't bother to listen. She didn't care what he had to say to his staff or the orders he gave. Someone else might have been bothered. She knew courtesans were often used as spies, but she was so far from that it was laughable. Unless, of course, there was a new breed of spy who couldn't wait to get as far away from her target as possible.

Her eyes traced the pattern in the silk overhead. If her five-year flight had taught her anything, it had taught her to consider every move before she made it. Escaping from Seth now, when she was on his ship, was going to be difficult, if not impossible, to accomplish.

She'd never been one to back down from a challenge.

Seth appeared in the doorway to interrupt her musings but came no farther. Jaida turned her head to look at him. He appeared ill at ease, his normally immaculate hair tousled across his broad shoulders and a frown on his face. Her heart twisted a little more, her determination not to show emotion fighting the need to go to him and smooth the frown from his brow.

Cold, emotionless, she reminded herself. Seth wasn't stupid; if she changed her attitude now, he was going to smell a rat. She rolled to her feet, wrapping the silk around her body toga style.

"My lord?" she asked, keeping her distance on the other side of the bed.

"I have to leave. We have a minor problem on the Alcarian border." His explanation was clipped as his silver eyes swept over her. Gone was the heat she'd seen earlier, replaced with a cold professional look.

A shiver ran up her spine. She'd seen that look before, right before he'd started to woo her. Determination rolled through her. If that was his game, then he was out of luck. She refused to let him get past her defenses again.

"You'll be comfortable in here," he said. "If you need anything else, all you have to do is comm me and I'll make sure you're tended to. Is there anything you'd like in particular?"

She cocked an eyebrow, and channelled her inner noble bitch. "My freedom?"

His chuckle was a rich burr of sound around the plush room. "That's the one thing you'll never get from me. Try again."

She shrugged. "Actually there is something…"

Seth looked at her in interest as he neared, his footsteps masked by the plush carpeting. Even without the carpet she wouldn't have heard his approach if he didn't want her to. He was a warrior prince, and went through the same harsh training as his men did.

"Name it, anything." His lips curved into a small, indulgent smile as he pulled her into his arms.

Jaida schooled herself to go quietly, reminding herself not to fight him. It was easier than she thought.

He pulled her closer, fitting her against the hard plains of his body as he studied her face. "So beautiful." He traced the line of her cheekbone, then her jaw with his fingertip. "I'll always look after you… give you anything your heart desires. Apart from your freedom."

The moment stretched between them, awareness and tension spiraling out of control. His fingertip traced her lips. The need to relax against him, rest her head on his shoulder, and agree to anything he wanted grew until it was nearly overwhelming.

She looked away. Submissive. Deferential.

"It's nothing much. I would like to use the hydroponics garden, please. If I recall, you have a temple to the Lady there… it's been a long time since I paid my respects in a proper temple."

She went for the jugular. It was his fault that she hadn't been able to pursue her faith at any of the mainstream temples. Any sighting of her would bring his men into town quicker than a market brought out bargain hunters.

As she expected, he winced but recovered quickly. "Of course. Feel free to wander this deck as you will. I would ask though that you do not try to enter any restricted areas. My guards can be somewhat vigilant in their duties and I wouldn't want you to get hurt by accident."

She inclined her head and extricated herself from his embrace as though his touch burned. "I wouldn't dream of it. I merely intend to spend my time in devotion."

Devotion to getting herself out of here, that was.

* * *

Less than an hour later, Jaida's plan was well under way.

None of the guards who accompanied her commented on her all-concealing red robe as they made their way to the hydroponic garden. She hadn't expected them to. Some men preferred their women covered up, which meant no one would guess she wasn't wearing the silk gown of a fallen woman underneath, but a fitted ship suit instead.

It was one of Seth's. In the black of Sector Seven,

it even had the unit insignia embroidered at the collar. It was too long and baggy from mid-thigh down and virtually painted on across her hips, but it made no difference to her what she looked like. She didn't plan on letting anyone see her wearing it and paired with the heaviest boots she could find, she was all set for her escape.

She nodded to the guards as they reached the hydroponics bay and swept inside with a regal swish of her robe, careful not to let the toes of her boots peek out.

Everything in the dressing rooms Seth had provided for her had been her size. Even the boots, designed for emergency evac situations. Why had he bothered? All the clothing she'd seen was expensive stuff, silks and satins from the far reaches of the galaxy. As much as men lavished gifts on their whores, it was a level of extravagance she hadn't expected. It was the kind of spending a man would reserve for his wife.

Pausing in the doorway she looked around the bay. Compared to the sterile steel and flexi-glass of the ship corridors, she'd stepped into a scene from a nature program. She took a deep breath and savored the moment.

A rolling lawn filled the space in front of her,

bordered by trees and formal gardens. The beds were filled with flowering plants but nestled within them there would be other varieties with more serious uses. Culinary herbs and pharmaceuticals The art and design of hydroponic gardens and ph'arming was something far beyond her.

She walked up the path to the small temple on the rise, pebbles crunching under her feet. If she didn't know better she could almost believe she was planet-side. The ceiling overhead was the finest flexi-glass, the support struts hidden, and she felt only the barest shimmer of a force field between her and the stars.

Jaida took a deep breath as she reached the marble columns of the temple at the top of the small hill. For a moment her plan was forgotten as she paused to center herself, allowing the tranquility of the temple to wash over her.

It had been so long since she'd prayed in a proper temple, even one of the huge public ones, and longer since she'd had the luxury of a private one. Most of the time she had to make do with an idol in the corner of her sleeping chamber. Silence surrounded her as she knelt before the altar, her knees pillowed by a purple velvet cushion.

"Lady in whom we place our trust..."

The familiar prayer was a balm to her wounded soul. Her lips formed the words by rote as the tang of the temple incense surrounded her, and she felt peace steal over her. Her lashes fluttered against her cheeks, then she opened her eyes and looked at the symbol in front of her on the wall. Three interlocking circles, the symbol of the mother-goddess, hung in hammered gold.

The same symbol was chiseled into the stone before her. As part of the ritual, her slender fingers traced the second circle in the group, that of the goddess in her fertile, motherly aspect rather than the circle of the maiden. She didn't worship the maiden aspect, not since she'd become a woman. *"… Lady's will be done."*

Her prayer finished, Jaida stood. Swift footsteps took her to doorway of the small temple, and she looked out to check if any of the guards had followed her in. She didn't expect any of them would have. One courtesan wasn't exactly a threat to a bunch of big, mean commandos. Her lips quirked in amusement. Courtesans were pampered and spoiled, their only duties to warm their master's beds and look pretty.

She stripped off the red robe and stuffed it under the altar. Pulling the altar cloth smooth, she looked at the scene again. Nothing out of place, it looked as though no one had been there. Good. She needed to conceal her movements and appearance for as long as possible. If they thought they were looking for a woman in a red robe, this would be so much easier.

There was only one door to the temple, the one she'd come in. As it was in full view of the hydroponic bay, leaving that way wasn't an option. Besides, the main bay was covered by the internal security net, so if she stepped out of here dressed like this, her cover was blown.

There had to be another way out, and she had an idea where to find it. Turning back, she fixed her gaze on the small windows to either side of the altar on the back wall. Hurrying over she swept the voile away from the narrow openings and leaned out over the wide ledge.

As expected, the temple structure backed onto the maintenance area. Below her, sheltered between the temple walls and concealing shrubs, were the pumps for the irrigation and sprinkler systems.

In the middle of the small recess was what she was looking for: an access hatch.

"Bingo."

She boosted herself onto the sill and wriggled through the window, then dropped down the other side. Her boots hitting the deck plating sounded like a gunshot. She froze in her crouch. The internal sensors had to have picked that up. Holding her breath, she waited for the thunder of feet heading toward her hiding place.

Long seconds passed, and the only thunder she heard was her own heart in her ears. Slowly she released the breath she'd been holding. For a brief second, hope filled her. She squashed it ruthlessly… she would make it or she wouldn't; hope had nothing to do with it. Hope just made her want things she shouldn't, and dream dreams she had no business even thinking about.

It only took her a few seconds to open the access hatch. Some thoughtful soul had scrawled the access code under the lock. She grinned as her fingers danced over the keypad; looked like someone had locked themselves out of the maintenance tubes one time too many.

As she climbed down, she lowered the hatch carefully back into place behind her. The lock slid back with a metallic *thunk* as she dropped the last couple of feet. Unlike the deck above, this one wasn't solid. The floor was made up of removable mesh panels suspended over the power lines, data cables, and other piping of the ship's systems. The lighting was luminescent cable running along the "ceiling". It was low level and dim, not enough to work by, but more than enough to see.

After a quick check along the corridor, she headed toward the shuttle bay. Her experiences while on the run had honed her sense of direction, so the twisting maze of tunnels posed no challenge. Before long she was kneeling behind a grate, looking at the entrance to the shuttle bay.

The *guarded* entrance to the shuttle bay.

Swearing under her breath, she drew back into the access tube. Two heavily built guards leaned either side of the double doors to the bay, right in her path. They looked bored as hell. One leaned against the wall, his head against the metal, while the other clicked coins from finger to finger, adding more each time. Curses filled the air when he lost control and the coins clattered across the corridor floor.

Crouched in the shaft she studied the problem from all sides and tried to work it out in her mind. How the hell was she going to get past them? She couldn't just walk past, and even though she knew how to take care of herself in a fight, these were Sector Seven commandos. They'd drop her to the floor and hog-tie her before she got the first punch in.

No, she needed an angle, the element of surprise, and a shitload of luck.

* * *

"I'm freaking bored, man."

Kelis sighed at the comment and concentrated on the coins he was flipping from finger to finger. He was up to five now and holding the rhythm. So far. He wasn't very good at it yet, but the chicks really dug it. Plus it beat whining like Tamrin.

"You're always bored, Tam."

"Well, are you surprised? We've been staring at this bit of corridor for the last five hours. I mean, I know we're 'protecting His Highness' and all that, but I hardly think they're gonna be stupid enough to try and get aboard a shuttle. That's like… breaking in through the front door or something."

Kelis flipped more coins. Tamrin had a point, but he wasn't going to admit that. They were Sector Seven, and the unit motto was "put up and shut up"… well, the unofficial one anyway. Officially there was a motto about death and honor and all that, but most S-Seven personnel did what they were told, when they were told, regardless of the order. It was what had gained them their fearful reputation with the rest of the galaxy. They were the baddest of the bad, and not even the Imadian pirates could match them.

"Yeah well, there was that serving girl who poisoned the wine at that ball the other month and the aristo's wife who tried with the stiletto. Actually she *did* come in through the front door, as I recall. Bitch was high on Tellaris root, needed seven to hold her. She was manic… it took that big bastard Jareth to take her down in the end."

"Yeah, he's freaking scary, man… those eyes. Manic like—what the *draanth* was that?"

Their heads whipped around as something clattered further down the hallway. In an instant both had pulse-pistols in their hands, eyes hard as they looked down the innocent looking corridor.

Kelis jerked his head toward the noise. Tamrin moved without a word, taking up a position on the other side of the corridor. Ghostlike, the two soldiers moved in the direction of the sound. It might just have been a coincidence, but Kelis didn't believe in coincidence.

Still, it might be something as simple as a loose access hatch banging, so he didn't call it in. Investigating with weapons drawn was more than enough. Despite what he'd said to Tamrin, this *was* the Prince's flagship. Anyone who tried anything would have to be insane, or suicidal. Or both. Yeah, definitely both.

Their footsteps were soundless on the deck plating. Their eyes were sharp, concentration complete, both pistols aimed and unwavering.

Kel grumbled silently as they moved down the corridor, moving in a leapfrog maneuver to cover each other. If this was just something mundane, they were going to look stupid. They hit the corner, Tamrin covering Kel as he rolled to the opposite wall and to his knees. Snapping his pistol up, he looked for the target.

The corridor was empty.

Kelis swore and jerked his pistol down out of the aimed position.

"*Draanth* it. We're clear. Those freaking engineers have left an access hatch loose again. I tell you man, I'm gonna bounce the duty chief for this. They've been told more than enough about this. You head back to the door, I'll fix this."

Kel stood and returned his pistol to the holster on his thigh with a vicious movement. Some engineer somewhere wasn't going to be able to hear for a week—hell, possibly ever again—when Kelis was done with him.

"Have fun with that." Tamrin didn't argue, just put his weapon up and turned on his heel.

"*Draanthing* engineers… If you want a job done, do it yourself," Kelis muttered under his breath as he headed for the open access hatch. It was slightly open, the heavy door resting just against the rim.

Kel knew what had happened. Someone had come through the hatch quickly and just slammed it shut without making sure the lock engaged. Sighing, he reached out for the edge of the hatch to close it when it flew open and slammed into his gut.

"Oof!"

The blow knocked Kelis off his feet. Breathless curses about defective equipment exploded from his mouth as he rolled to his knees. He didn't see the booted feet that emerged out of the open hatch behind him, or the crowbar that crashed down on the back of his combat helmet.

Thump… thud. Jaida winced as the guard went down. Had she hit him too hard? She didn't want to hurt anyone, just get the hell out of here. Placing the crowbar within easy reach, she knelt by the fallen guard, and pushed her fingertips to his neck between the high collar and his helmet.

Relief flooded through her as his pulse beat strongly under her fingers. He was okay, but he'd have a hell of a headache when he woke up. She almost felt sorry for him. Conscience assuaged, she reached down and pulled the heavy pistol from its holster. Her movements were quick and precise as she checked the safety and the settings, betraying her hard won experience with weaponry. Lips pressed together, she set it to heavy stun and turned. Time to deal with the second guard.

On silent feet she padded to the corner and crouched to peep around it, her purloined pistol held loosely in her hand. Luck was with her. The second guard was kneeling halfway along the corridor, tying his shoelaces. Jaida shook her head. It didn't seem possible that these two were from Seth's elite guard.

Praise the Lady for bored soldiers.

Silently she rose and stepped out from the corner. She raised the pistol and aimed. She moved her finger and clicked the laser sight on. A red dot appeared in the middle of the guard's back. It wasn't strictly necessary for the stun setting she was using but given the fact this guy was Sector

Seven, she couldn't afford to miss. He was the only thing that stood between her and a shuttle to freedom.

She pulled the trigger and watched as he slumped to the ground. She flicked a glance up, noting the security camera. It swept the corridor in a continuous arc. Even if she managed to keep out of its line of sight, someone would notice the unconscious guards. If she wanted to make it out of here, she was going to have to be fast.

Her hair swung about her shoulders as she checked behind her. She hadn't expected to get this far, and every moment she expected to find armed men behind her.

Her lips compressed in determination. If she made it, then this time, she would get so far away he'd never find her, perhaps even the Imadian expanse. The place was riddled with pirate holdouts and fraught with clan wars, but it was the one place he'd never look for her.

First though, she had to get off this damn ship. Pistol held loosely by her side she trotted down the corridor toward the shuttle bay doors. Since she wasn't wearing a suppression bracelet like the guards, the doors detected her life signs and slid open silently. She ducked to one side, just in case there were more guards inside, and then slowly peeked around the edge of the door.

Row upon row of sleek fighters and shuttlecraft met her eyes. At the other end of the cavernous room, deckhands and mechanics milled about. That wasn't a problem; she didn't intend to head down to that end of the bay.

She slid through the door on silent feet and took cover behind the nearest fighter. Her gaze was fixed on the shuttle bay launch doors. Opening like a massive maw, it was all that separated the bay from cold space, along with the faint shimmer of a force field. The deckhands weren't going to be her biggest challenge; getting through that field was.

CHAPTER 5

"*What?*"

Seth looked at his second in command in utter disbelief.

"Okay, let me get this straight. We're on the flagship of the royal fleet, a ship literally crawling with commandos, and you're telling me one small woman... one small, *unarmed* woman... managed to escape?"

General Jareth Nikolai, the Prince's second in command, looked right back. He didn't flinch, nor did he avoid Seth's gaze. His voice was blunt and to the point as he replied. "Yes, your majesty. She went into the hydroponics bay at fifteen twenty-three to use the temple. As per your instructions two guards were posted on the doors at all times. At fifteen forty-five the guard was changed, and the bay was checked. That was when we discovered the guards on the main launch bay doors were unconscious and Lady Jaida was missing. The security cameras on the bay doors are on a slow sweep pattern, so we can only assume it was her."

Seth ran his hand through his hair in exasperation, sweeping it back from his face. "*Draanth.*"

"Yeah. That just about covers it." Jareth's voice held a hint of quiet amusement that made Seth lift his head quickly. As usual Jareth's face was stoic. An expression Seth knew well.

"Okay, out with it... before you bust a gut laughing."

Jareth gave him a blank look. "Huh? Me?"

His blue-black eyes were wide and innocent, but Seth knew him of old. They'd met the first day of basic training, beaten the crap out of each other, and been firm friends ever since. The commoner and the prince, the two most feared men in the princedom.

"I've got nothing to say."

Seth blew out a sigh of frustration and resisted the temptation to slap his friend upside the ear. For one, it wasn't very dignified on the bridge of an imperial battle cruiser, and for two, Seth couldn't remember the last time he'd managed to land a blow on the other man without the element of surprise or an excessive amount of alcohol.

"So, she's been missing twenty-two minutes. Where the hell could she have gone?" Seth turned and dropped down in the command chair. It had taken him years to find her, and now, in the space of hours, she'd managed to elude him again.

"Some refreshment, your majesty?"

A voice broke through Seth's musings. He opened his eyes to find Warin hovering solicitously at his side, a small tray containing a jug of water and a crystal goblet in his hands. Behind the manservant, Jareth's face was set in dislike, or as near to the expression as the general would allow in public. Seth sighed; as much as he'd tried to persuade Warin not to hover like a puppy dog, the words seemed to go in one ear and out the other.

"No, thank you, Warin. Please, you should be off duty now."

"Oh, very kind of Your Highness, but my greatest pleasure in life is to serve." Warin flushed bright red at Seth's direct comment and bowed so low Seth was sure he was going to go head over heels on the deck plating.

"Be that as it may, but I really do need my favorite servant well rested. Can't have you off duty with exhaustion, can we?" Seth smiled and stood, towering over the shorter man. Warin backed up, muttering apologies at being in the prince's personal space.

"No problem," Seth clapped the man on the shoulder, not really seeing him anymore as he looked over at Jareth and rolled his eyes. "Off you go, get some sleep."

"Thank you kindly, Sire." Warin turned to go but stopped after a few steps and looked over his shoulder. There was a strange expression on his face, somewhere between determination and need.

"Your Majesty, if I might be so bold? She's not worth it. There are many far more deserving of y-y-your... " The servant stuttered to a halt and dropped his gaze, the flush on his cheeks going from light pink to fire-red. "... far more deserving of your affections, your majesty."

Seth's eyebrow winged up. Silence fell over the bridge at the servant's words, a silence so profound that not only would he have been able to hear a pin drop, but he'd also have been able to work out the length and diameter of the thing as well.

"Yes... Thank you for your opinion, Warin." Seth's voice was formal and restrained. "I shall not need you until the morning. Dismissed."

Seth turned back to Jareth, who watched Warin walk across the bridge, not speaking until the doors slid shut behind him.

"That man is a snake in the grass."

"He's not so bad. Forgets his place at times, I must admit. Minor son of a noble lord, so I guess that's understandable."

Jareth caught his arm as he walked by, stopping his progress and looking at him directly. "Just watch your back, my friend. Something about him doesn't ring true."

Surprised, Seth just nodded. It was rare for Jareth to venture such a strong opinion on someone. So rare that, had it been anyone but Warin, Seth would have been inclined to listen to him. But this was his manservant… for heaven's sake, he'd served Seth for years. And he had access to Seth's room when he slept. If he was a danger, Seth was sure he'd have found out by now.

"I'll watch him. I'm sure you're wrong, but I'll watch him. Happy?"

Jareth released his arm and went back to his console. "Of course, always am. You know me."

"Yeah, you're a regular bundle of joy and happiness." Seth sat back down and rubbed the bridge of his nose between his fingers to soothe the headache that was beginning to form. So many things were going around in his skull he was sure it was going to explode soon.

He'd seen the look in Jaida's eyes when he'd found her. Fear... that was to be expected... after all she had run from the most powerful man in the princedom for years, but there had been something else as well.

Longing perhaps. For him? He'd assumed so at the time.

"Draanthing hell ... "

"Excuse me?" Jareth's voice broke into his thoughts.

"Nothing, carry on." He waved his hand in dismissal, locked in his thoughts. "Find her!"

He'd read her wrong. It hadn't been longing. It had been exhaustion. A tiredness so complete it had suppressed the sparkling wit and spirit that had hooked him in the first place. For the first time in years, Seth felt unsure. This Jaida wasn't the young girl who'd looked at him with adoration. This Jaida was a woman with strength and resourcefulness, a woman he didn't know...

A raucous sound pierced the silence of the bridge, the harsh tone cutting through all activity for a second.

Seth lifted his head and Jareth paused retracing his steps back onto the bridge. Both men looked toward the security officer.

"Report," Seth barked, sitting upright in his seat as Jareth came to stand at his shoulder, the traditional place for the Ship's Second. "Unauthorized launch sir, from the primary shuttle bay."

"Get me a feed, put it on the holo."

The security officer nodded, and a moment later a flickering screen appeared suspended in midair before the raised command dais. The two men watched as a fighter patrol flew into the bay in formation and smoothly touched down. Perfect landings as far as Seth could see.

"Play it back, reduce speed by half," Jareth ordered, his eyes sharp as he rounded Seth's chair to get closer to the screen. "Here, see? Bottom right of the screen. A shuttle slips out just as the field drops for the last fighter."

He turned to Seth, admiration on his face for a moment before he blanked his expression. "Whoever is piloting that shuttle, they've got split second timing. We could do with more pilots like that. You think it's our girl?"

Seth shook his head but he knew the answer. It

was Jaida; there was no one else it could be. Where had she learned to fly like that?

"Has to be. She had to have had help, there's no way a woman raised as a noble would fly like that." His voice was curt as he stood. "Ready my shuttle, we're going after her."

Two hours later Seth was growling and gritting his teeth as he chased down the fleeing shuttle. In a straight run, Jaida's shuttle had no chance against the sleek craft Seth piloted. Which was the reason she'd made straight for the asteroid field at the edge of the system. At first he'd thought she'd enlisted help. Perhaps bribed someone on the ship. But the sensors aboard the Prince's Dream were top of the range and only read one bio-sign aboard the escaped shuttle. It was Jaida herself trying to lose him in a dizzying race of twists and turns as they barreled through the scattered asteroids and space debris.

"You are one *crazy* lady."

He cursed as she performed another hard turn. A few more seconds and she would have ended up a sticky mess against the side of a rock. Shooting a quick prayer to the Lady Goddess, Seth hit the same hard turn. The sound of tortured metal filled the cockpit as his wing tip scraped along the surface of the rock. An inch more and he'd have ripped the wing clean off. His jaw tightened in determination, his eyes unwavering on the shuttle dodging and weaving in front of him.

"No way out princess, you know that." All he needed was a clear gap in the asteroid field to hit the engines and get above her, then he could activate the mag-locks and haul her in. She knew it, he knew it.

The trick though, was getting above her. As the two craft dodged and wove in a high-speed version of cat and mouse, the prince was pushed to the limit to keep up with his quarry.

"Seth, will you just draanth off and die?"

Jaida swore and hit the brakes to slow the hurtling shuttle. It all but stood on its nose, everything loose in the cabin sliding to the front of the craft. She didn't bother to reach out and move the mess. Instead, she looked around a half-filled maintenance report form, and slammed her flight controls hard left. Responsive to the slightest twitch of her fingers, the small craft went into a tight barrel roll.

Keeping one eye on the view ahead of her to

avoid a fatal collision with an asteroid she kept the other on the controls. The tiny blip on her console that was Seth's shuttle shot off to the right, following her original course.

"Woohoo! You fell for it. Sucker!" She whooped in triumph. He'd missed the turn, and from her sensor readings, the field was too dense for him to loop back now. He'd have to exit the asteroid field before finding a way back in to come look for her. "And by that time *kelarris* I'll be long gone."

Gritting her teeth in determination, she lowered her head and concentrated on the obstacle course ahead. She gunned the engines, flipping and weaving through the boulders and space debris in a break-neck race for freedom.

This was insane. No one in their right mind would see an asteroid field like this as a viable escape route. She didn't either, but her escape wasn't the asteroid field itself. Once she was free and clear of it, it would be pretty easy for Seth to catch her. The shuttle she'd chosen wasn't built for speed, but maneuverability. He had the bigger, more powerful shuttle, so one good boost on the burners and he'd be all over her like a bad rash.

If she was still about when he got clear of the field, that was. The rocks ahead of her started to thin out. Boulders the size of small moons gave way to smaller versions, and smaller yet, until the rubble that surrounded her was no bigger than a football. Her slender fingers danced over the console as she ramped the shields up to full, preparing to blast through the remainder.

Already her eyes were focused on her goal. Beyond the field was the most beautiful sight she'd ever seen: the meandering iridescent blue turbulence of a naturally occurring jump-field.

Freedom.

Natural jump fields were rare. So rare there were only thirteen recorded and all of them were heavily guarded to stop dirty little outlaws like her from using them to escape justice. Once inside a jump field, a person could go anywhere in the galaxy, provided they had the coordinates. Or they could simply jump from field to field, not exiting until they got where they wanted. Or they could hop off at the farthest point and simply disappear.

Because security was so tight, she'd never even tried to get near one. With so many agencies on the lookout for her, trying to stow away on any of the commercial liners was a no-go. She'd have been picked up in seconds. She'd kicked the idea about for months, trying to figure a way to get aboard one.

Once on board, all she had to do was locate an emergency pod and *bam,* she was home clear. Even the meager landing thrusters on a pod would enable her to navigate in the ebbs and flows of the jump stream.

All her plotting and planning had come to nothing though. With retinal and DNA scans standard procedure at all jump-stations, there was no way for a wanted woman to get anywhere near check in, never mind departures.

All fields were heavily guarded, even this one. It had patrols and automated level-six defense drones on all sides. Bar one—the side covered by an "impenetrable" asteroid field. Jaida allowed a small smile to cross her lips as she set a direct course for the shimmering violet-blue of freedom.

Clunk-click. Slam.

The sound of metal on metal sounded overhead and reverberated through the small shuttlecraft. She jumped, wincing at the tortured scream of the shuttle's space frame as something latched onto it. Mag locks.

"Shit! No! This isn't happening."

Her gaze raced over the pilots' consoles. Her hands followed suit, but she knew it was hopeless. Something large and powerful had locked onto her with clamps, the high magnetic fields starting to disrupt the smaller vessel's systems as it was reeled in.

"No, no, no. I won't go back… I can't go back."

Tearing her harness off, she was out of the pilot's chair in a second. Desperation hummed through her frame as she looked around the small cabin. The shuttle was two man, with one interior room and no escape pod. A single low-rise bulkhead separated the cockpit from the tiny living area.

Her eyes widened as a new sound entered the fray directly overhead; a grinding, squealing noise. As she watched, the ceiling began to glow in a distinctive circle. Instinctively she ducked as the sparks of the boarding-cutter began to fly.

She backed up into the corner, tears of anger and frustration pricking at the back of her eyes. She'd been so close… so close she could almost smell freedom. Her gaze latched onto the glowing, spitting circle in the roof as she slid down the wall into a tired, defeated little ball. Hopelessness rose up to overwhelm her. She would never be free of him.

Ever.

The boarding cutter was almost done. Seth stood by the machine and waited impatiently as it did its work, cutting through the layers of high-tensile steel and tri-titanium plates which made up the hull of Jaida's shuttle.

It would be ruined, of course, but once he had her aboard the *Prince's Dream* he'd cut it loose to become just another piece of debris in the asteroid field. It wouldn't take long for random collisions with the rocks within to render it unidentifiable and its technology too smashed to be useful to anyone.

Finally the cutter was done. His jaw tightened as it snapped off. Gas hissed as it was released and the air pressure between the two vessels equalized. An old hand at boarding other ships, Seth swallowed and wiggled his jaw until his ears popped. With a whir the laser ring lifted and withdrew back into its recess, taking the section it had cut from the shuttle below with it.

He approached the hatch with care, scooting down to look around the compartment revealed below. She was armed, or at least she had been on his flagship if the empty holsters of the incapacitated guards were any indication. The last thing he wanted was to dangle his legs through there and get shot in the family jewels.

His hair brushed the deck plating as he lowered his body into a push-up position to get a view of the back of the shuttle. Grease and whatever they used to clean the plasti-flooring wafted up to his nose as he scooted around.

His eyes narrowed. She was in the back corner, curled up into a ball with her arms around her legs and her head on her knees. He frowned. What in blazes was she doing?

Checking the restraining clip on his sidearm Seth dropped through the hatch and landed lightly. He kept his eyes on her all the time in case she went for a weapon. She didn't move. She didn't even flinch as his boots hit the deck plating.

"Jaida?"

There was no reply. In fact, she didn't respond at all as he walked toward her, and he was left in the unusual position of not knowing what the hell to do. Where were the pistols she'd taken? With half an eye on the seated woman, he cast his gaze about the cabin, finally locating them in the foot well in front of the copilot's seat. His frown deepened. Nothing about this was making sense. Why would she run again, and not use them when he caught her?

"Jaida, *kelarris*… are you hurt?"

He crossed the cabin in long strides. Worried, he searched for signs of blood. The madcap moves she'd been pulling could easily have thrown her from the pilot's seat and knocked her out.

"I'm not hurt."

Her voice was quiet, and finally she moved. Her hand disappeared under the fall of her hair and he got the distinct impression she was wiping her eyes dry.

"Look at me."

Crouching in front of her, he tried to see under the cascading purple locks. He was expecting to see teary eyes filled with the tiredness he'd seen earlier. What he wasn't expecting was for her to burst into action. In his haste to make sure she was okay he hadn't noticed how she was sat, with her legs half bunched under her.

Big mistake.

Using the power from her coiled legs she threw herself at him, knocking him off his feet, and heading for the cut-out boarding hatch that led to his craft.

"What the—" Seth swore as he landed on his ass. Her slender, lithe form shot over him, just out of reach of his grasping hands. He twisted, forcing his body into movement. If she got through that hatch and hit the disengage switch, he was going to be sucking cold space. The fact that Jaida would be put to death for the murder of an Imperial Prince was scant comfort. He'd still be dead.

She reached the hatch, leaped up and dangled from it as she prepared to haul herself into the shuttle above.

"Oh no you don't." Adrenalin surged through him as he threw himself toward her. She squealed, a soft exclamation of denial and frustration as she tried to haul herself out of the way. He hit her midsection and they fell from the hatch in a tangle of limbs.

Seth found himself holding onto a wildcat. Someone, somewhere, had taught Jaida to fight. His breath left his lungs in a hiss as he blocked rapid-fire punches. She didn't hit hard, but she was *fast*, and good as he was, some sneaked through his guard.

"You little—"

After what seemed like an age, he latched a hand around one of her slender wrists and slammed it into the deck above her head. His lips compressed into a hard line as he grabbed the other one and forced it to join the first.

"What the draanth did you think you were doing?" He glared down at her, but she wouldn't look at him. Her eyes remained closed tight and her face turned away. He was too angry at first to notice the way her body felt under his, the way her curves fitted to his hard planes, but that didn't last long.

His cock hardened in a heartbeat, a fact that just fueled his anger. Warin was right; there were other women who would welcome his love, yet he wanted the one who'd run. She'd tried to kill him… and he still wanted her.

What kind of sick bastard was he?

CHAPTER 6

"*Look* at me!" The hard grip on her wrists brought tears to her eyes. "You were going to condemn me to cold, hard space so the least you can do is look at me."

Jaida felt the flames of Seth's anger licking at her skin as he hauled her to her feet. Even if she had gotten into his shuttle, she hadn't a clue what she'd been going to do. She'd run out of desperation, but she hadn't meant to kill him. Not even to save her own life, not even if it meant she could escape him forever. She'd never have done that.

"No. No... I wasn't. I swear!"

For once she didn't fight him, just lifted her eyes to his. Pleading with him. She needed him to believe that. For some reason deep inside, she couldn't bear that he thought she could do something like that.

"Can it."

His voice was as hard as his hands as he pulled her upright and spun her around. Air exploded from her lungs in a cry as he twisted her arm up her back. A firm grip held her wrist painfully high between her shoulder blades and the sound of him searching in his pockets came from behind her. An agonizing ache throbbed through her captured arm. All she could do was stand there and concentrate on breathing. Even the tiniest move sent fresh waves of agony through her body.

"Please," she whimpered, hating herself for the pathetic note in her voice, but begging anyway. "You're hurting me."

Coldness clamped around her wrists, first the one up her back, then when he released it, around the other. Jaida couldn't focus for a moment; a bone-cracking jolt of pain surged through her body as he released the pressure on her wrist.

She staggered forward, catching herself on the single cot at the side of the compartment and hugging her abused arm close to her body. Long seconds later the pain subsided, and she could breathe again.

"What the hell was that?" Instinctively she rubbed her hands down her arms and paused as she encountered something new. Around her wrists were two narrow metal cuffs. "What the—"

"That was a Terranian pressure hold."

He yanked her to her feet and pushed her toward the hole in the ceiling. "And those are neural restraint cuffs," he said, bundling her through the boarding hatch as though she weighed nothing. She squeaked as she flew through the air, his hands getting very familiar with her butt. Too familiar.

Then she hit the hard deck plating of the shuttle above. She still had enough wits about her to try and scramble away and put as much distance between herself and Seth's anger as she could.

"Oh no you don't. Cuffs, mag-hold."

Seth's order was sharp as he hauled himself up after her. The bracelets on her wrists yanked her arms down until she was forced to her hands and knees. The metal of the cuffs clicked against the deck plating and stuck.

Grunting with effort Jaida yanked on them but they refused to budge. Sticking her ass in the air, she put one foot against the floor next to her wrists and heaved.

"Son of a *bitch*!" she cursed as she managed to

take three layers of skin off the inside of her wrists. "Seth. You let me out of here, right now!"

His laughter rolled around the cabin as he walked past her and her upturned ass. It wasn't a nice sound. There was no humor and lots of bitterness in it. She shivered and dropped to her knees, shuffling around to keep him in sight. Ignoring her, he worked at the main console, his tall broad-shouldered form blocking the view out the main window.

Behind her the boarding mechanism whirred into action. Metal grated against metal in a high pitched and tortured squeal as the hatch started to move.

"Hope you didn't have anything valuable on there."

The view of the other shuttle's interior disappeared. A heavy thud reverberated through the small vessel as the docking clamps disengaged. The floor lurched on release, and Jaida's knees slid across the floor. The cuffs rubbed another layer of skin from the inside of her wrists before she could brace herself and stop her movement.

"If you did, tough shit. It's gone."

Wariness hummed through her body as he turned toward her. For a moment she was caught up in just watching him. He didn't walk; he stalked.

Every movement held the grace and beauty of a warrior in his prime. A predator. One with all his attention focused on her. She'd spent five years running from his wrath, but in that instant, she realized she'd never seen him this angry.

Anger swirled around him like a storm, fury and frustration rolling off him in waves as he approached. Her heart stilled in her chest as he stood over her. His silver eyes were hard as he studied her. Seconds crawled by and stretched out to occupy centuries. She searched his eyes, looking for something, anything, but they were devoid of expression. Shuffling back, she tried to put distance between them, only to be stopped by the cuffs on her wrists.

"Damn it! Let me out of... " She didn't get to finish her demand. He sliced his hand up for silence.

"You wanted to be treated as a whore?" His voice was cold as ice as he reached down to grab her wrist.

"Well, I didn't me—"

"I'll tell you when I want you to speak. Mag-release."

His hand was on her arm, hauling her upright before she could take another breath. He let go but didn't move away, just stood so close she could feel the heat of his body beating against hers. Warily she lifted her gaze to his. Heat and intent burned in the silver depths.

She swallowed and backed up. For each step she took backward, he took one forward, stalking her across the cabin. Her flight stopped when her shoulders bumped against the metal bulkhead of the wall.

"Nowhere left to go, Jaida."

His voice was low, almost seductive, but with a core of steel. She shivered at the sound. Her heart thumped painfully against her ribcage as he stepped toward her. His hand stroked down her shoulder and slid down her arm until he reached her wrist. Gently he captured one hand then the other, stretching them over her head. Any choice was just illusion. She didn't dare move or argue for fear of bringing his wrath down on her. The cuffs clicked against the metal wall and she knew what was coming before he spoke.

"Cuffs, mag-lock"

Jaida tried to keep the tears from her eyes. She didn't want this, not with him angry with her. Hard hands skimmed over her figure in a hard caress. One paused in the curve of her waist as the other reached down and hooked the back of her knee. Lifting her leg, he pulled it over his hip and pressed into her. She caught her breath as the thick hardness of his cock rubbed against her. Even with the layers of clothing between them, the friction and pressure against her hypersensitive clit almost had her eyes rolling back in her head.

"You keep telling me you're a whore, so you win. I'll treat you like one. I'm fed up with treating you like a lady and getting it thrown back in my face. Whores get screwed, which suits me just fine."

Her heart ached at his cruel words. Then his hands were moving over her body and scattering her thought processes, cruel hard caresses as he explored the curves and lines of her body, ones that made her burn with shame… and squirm with need.

"We don't need this. Whores don't wear clothes."

His hand caught in the neck of her suit and tore it down the front in one savage move. Cool air washed over skin as he shoved the fabric out of the way to reveal her body from neck to crotch. She squirmed, her breasts jiggling as she realized he could see everything. Heat surged through her as she saw herself as he must see her.

Arms above her head, bare breasts rising and falling with each breath as her nipples tightened into tight little buds begging for attention. The softness of her belly as it gave way to the neatly trimmed triangle of hair over her mound just visible at the end of the tear.

"Of course," he continued, his voice hard, but his eyes hotter than a star going supernova. "Wearing this adds another black mark to your already impressive record."

He shook his head then reached out and tweaked one of her nipples. Liquid heat flooded her body, slipping from her pussy as it made itself ready for him. Her face burned with shame.

"Impersonating a Sector Seven operative is a serious offense. By rights I should have you thrown in prison."

His fingers slid under the last bit of fabric covering her modesty and pulled. The fabric gave again, this time the tear going all the way along the seam, only stopping halfway up, just below her tailbone. Jaida whimpered. She was completely open to him and helpless. He could do whatever he wanted to her now. Who was she kidding? From that moment in the dockyard office he'd been able to do anything he wanted to her.

He kissed down her neck, but the touch of his lips panicked rather than aroused her. Tears welled in her eyes and spilled down her cheeks unchecked. She didn't care that he saw, didn't care what he thought anymore, whether he thought she was weak or pathetic or not. She didn't want this, and every kiss with no feeling in it that he placed on her skin broke her heart.

SETH REACHED up to brush her hair back from her face and claim her lips. His fingers encountered wetness and he frowned. She was crying.

He froze, his heart twisting painfully.

Silent tears streamed down her cheeks; her head turned away from him. Lady, what kind of monster was he? He'd never forced a woman before, especially not one who meant as much to him as Jaida.

"Oh Lady... I'm sorry. Mag-release."

As soon as the cuffs released, Seth gathered her up into his arms and carried her to the bed. Her suit was ruined but her hands fluttered around the torn front, trying to pull it back together and cover her nakedness. Seth tried to help, only to have her flinch from his touch.

"No, no. I can do it," she muttered, her voice thick with tears.

He stood up, unsure of what to do. She flinched when he touched her, fear and pain in her eyes. Even in his blackest rages, he hadn't wanted that. Not for her to fear him and dread his touch.

"Here."

He tried to make his voice as gentle as possible as he recovered a blanket from the compartment above the bed and draped it over her. She pulled it around her like a shield and drew her legs up close. Her shoulders shook harder, the sobs still silent, as though she'd learned not to show her pain to the world.

Seth winced, feeling every silent sob like a spear to his heart. What had he done? Was his revenge worth this? Worth breaking completely? He'd never wanted this. Unable to stand by idly he sat down on the bunk next to her and pulled her into his arms.

"Hey hey, *kelarris,* I'm not going to hurt you."

She struggled against him, her body rigid with panic. He soothed her with soft murmurs, holding her tightly against him to quell her struggles. It didn't take much. Within thirty seconds she whimpered and turned toward him.

He leaned back against the wall at the back of the bunk and cradled her in his lap. His hand stroked down her back as she cried, his lips against her hair as he sang half-remembered lullabies from his childhood. Eventually her sobs slowed, and then stopped, leaving just the occasional hiccup.

After a while, Seth lifted his head. Her breathing had deepened and leveled out. A soft smile curved his lips. She was asleep. With careful movements, he shifted their positions on the narrow bunk, tucking her along the back wall still wrapped in the blanket. He left her to set the shuttle into a parallel orbit pattern with the asteroid belt and radio in.

Less than four minutes later, he slid into the bunk next to her and gathered her into his arms again. This time, even in sleep, she came willingly and nestled against him with a sigh. A deep sense of contentment stole over Seth, and he closed his eyes.

He was home.

* * *

SHE WAS DREAMING. Again. It was a dream that got trotted out with alarming regularity, so she recognized it as soon as she slipped into it. It was always the same, waking up to find herself held against a broad male chest and feeling safe. Feeling like nothing in the galaxy could hurt her because he loved her. He, of course, was never defined. In her dream she never opened her eyes. She preferred to dwell in the fantasy and try to hold onto it as long as possible.

As dreams went it wasn't particularly ambitious, just a strong pair of arms to hold her, attached to a man who loved her and cared for her. For Jaida it was the one thing she could never have, and she knew it. Seth had pursued her across the length and breadth of the galaxy. She feared what he'd do to *her* when he caught her, so what he'd do to any man she'd taken up with was something she didn't like to think about.

She nestled closer and took a deep breath. The alluring scent of the man she was wrapped around filled her senses. The clean, sharp scent of a citrus-based shower gel, the heavier musk of altarian sandalwood, all combined with an earthy deep fragrance that had to be the man himself. She murmured happily and buried her nose against a chest that felt like satin stretched over carved granite.

It wasn't just the fact Seth would most likely kill any guy she was with, though. In the safety of her dreams, she could admit the secret yearnings of her heart, even if she couldn't admit them while awake. The reason she'd never so much as looked at another guy was because she was like her father; once she'd fallen in love, it had been for life.

She sighed as a large hand stroked her back. She was in love with Seth. She could even admit *that* here in the sanctuary of her dreams. His response last night when he realized she was crying was like something straight out of one of her dreams.

She ignored the fact he'd made her cry in the first place The fact that he'd stopped when he did, as angry as he was, meant everything to her. As much as he seemed to hate her, there had to be something there—even if it was just the common decency of one sentient being to another.

She must have drifted off to sleep again in her dream, because the next thing she knew, warm lips were trailing down her throat. She froze, then relaxed as the familiar scent of her dream man assaulted her senses again. It was okay, this was just part of her dream. Admittedly a new and—she shivered in delight —intriguing part of the dream, but still a dream.

Warm lips whispered over her skin, finding all the spots that made her whimper in delight. Murmuring softly, she turned her head to allow him better access. It felt so good, so right, she couldn't resist. Couldn't do anything but urge her dream lover on as a large, callused hand slid under the warm blankets and encountered her naked skin beneath.

His hand stroked up her ribcage inch by slow inch. Her back arched in welcome, her breasts tightening and firming, and her nipples puckering into tight buds as though to invite his touch. He cupped one of them, full despite her slenderness, and rolled the nipple between his fingers.

She gasped, not expecting that. Always in her dreams before, her lover had been romantic and... old-fashioned to a fault. A whimper escaped her lips as he trailed a line of hot kisses down her neck and farther. Leaning down, he swirled a hot tongue over her nipple, and then sucked it into his mouth. Her gasp was nearer a keen this time. Her eyes rolled back in her head as he sucked hard on the engorged bud. Fire drew a line directly between the warmth of his mouth on her sensitive flesh and the ache building in her pussy. With each tug on her nipple, her inner channel contracted tightly. Wanting, no *aching*, to be filled.

He swept his tongue over her nipple again then moved down. The warmth of his breath whispered over her stomach as he left a trail of butterfly kisses over her quivering skin. Normally she was ticklish, but not here, not now. The muscles of her stomach tightened in arousal as he paid homage to the slight indentation of her belly button, then moved on to nibble along the blade of her hipbone.

She bit her lip to contain the moan that welled up from her soul. She couldn't bear this much longer. His lips hovered for a moment over the small triangle of hair at her mons. Twitching in anticipation her clit ached as she imagined his warm, wet mouth closing over her.

His tongue swept over her folds, tentative at first. An exploratory sweep. He stilled for a moment as his tongue encountered the smooth skin of her labia, the hair removed as per the more intimate preparations in the harem chambers. Why that bit had carried over into her dream she didn't know, but right at this moment, she didn't care.

He rumbled in approval, the low noise from deep within his chest. The next pass of his tongue parted the outer lips and sought the sweetness inside. Sweeping lightly from her cunt upwards he found the small nubbin of flesh aching for his touch and closed over it.

He sucked it into his mouth. She swore as her hips bucked, the curse straight off the dockyard, the touch of his tongue like an electric shock that made her back arch in response.

His hand spread over her stomach to hold her in place for the attentions of his mouth. He didn't just taste her, gathering the juices of her arousal from the entrance to her pussy with another rumble. No, he feasted on her.

Holding her clit between his teeth he flicked rapidly over it with his tongue then alternated with suckling hard. Her head thrashed on the pillow as pressure built into a tight coil within her. She tried to deny the need gathering force inside.

"Oh lady…"

Her dreams had never been this vivid and graphic before. Ever. Everything was sharper and more focused than the vaguely romantic and safe cuddling-in-bed dream she was used to. His tongue flicked over her again then stabbed deep into her pussy, a hard thrust that had her whimpering aloud.

The knowledge that this wasn't a dream hovered at the edge of her mind for a while before she allowed herself to process the information. She opened her eyes, looking up at the metal ceiling of the shuttle.

Seth. Who else could possibly bring her this much pleasure? What other man had brought her body to life, could bring her body to life in this way?

What other man would have been the faceless lover of her dreams? Too close to the edge to stop him, even though she knew she should, Jaida surrendered to the inevitable and the pleasure he afforded her.

His lips pulled on her clit again and then he circled with his tongue. Her breath came in short pants as her world focused solely on the sensations he created. Another lick and she was there. Her climax rose, roaring in her ears like the thunder of a waterfall. Everything slowed as she hovered on the very edge. Waiting. Just one more lick, one more touch.

He pulled away. She whimpered in distress. Shoved her hips toward him. He couldn't leave her like this, not on the very edge of release. His chuckle was soft, but he didn't make her wait long. His tongue swept over her clit as he drove two thick fingers inside her.

"Oh... *oh...* " she moaned as an orgasm closed around her, wrapping her in its white-hot embrace. Her hips pumped mechanically as waves of pleasures rolled through her. Her pussy clenched tight around his invading fingers as she rode them, too mindless to think of anything else but her own release.

. . .

Lady, she was going to be the death of him. Seth bit back his own moan as Jaida came apart under his hands and lips. The sweet scent of her release surrounded him like the finest perfume. Her tight inner channel clenching around his fingers was pure torture. All he could think about was ripping his pants open, freeing his cock and driving into her to reach heaven.

She was his addiction and his cure all rolled into one. Bitter amusement twisted Seth's lips. It figured she would be the one woman who hated his guts. The goddess had a mean streak.

Sitting back on his heels, he watched her. Spread out over the bunk in front of him, just on the edge of sleep with the ship-suit open to reveal her voluptuous figure, she was an image out of any red-blooded male's fantasy.

She was the only image in his. When he'd woken with her in his arms, he hadn't been able to resist kissing her. For years he'd fantasized about this, about what would happen when he finally got her back. His mind had conjured up all sorts of fantasies. Everything from a romantic reconciliation with her declaring she was wrong, to nastier scenes where he had her tied, bound, and gagged as he screwed her.

His fingers stroked gently over her G-spot, her

moans soft on the air. But he would never just screw her. Nothing so crude. They would always make love, even if she didn't realize it. There had never been any other way for him. Not with her.

She came down slowly. With a flush on her cheeks, she opened her eyes and looked at him. Her eyes were midnight velvet, warm and unfocused from her pleasure. He bit back a groan as he nearly came there and then. Goddess, she was beautiful.

Gently he pulled from her. His hand shook as he released himself. The thick shaft of his cock leapt from its fabric confinement into his hand. He stroked himself, long slow movements as he watched her, looking for some sign she didn't want this. Precum leaked from the tip of his cock. Sweeping a finger over the broad head, he spread it over his length.

Gaze riveted on her he moved forward. His cock in hand, he angled it to press against the slick entrance to her body. Rotating his hips, he teased her, gratified when she moaned again, the breathy sounds filling the cabin and driving him mad.

If there was any doubt about how much she wanted this, they were all swept away as she bit her lip and pushed against him. His breath caught in his chest as he slipped inside her half an inch.

He was in heaven.

A low moan tore from his chest as he slid deep inside her, a slow, long, wet ride of unbelievable pleasure. She was as tight and hot as he remembered. Her pussy closed around him and accepted him in a tight embrace that had him swelling impossibly further. He was painfully hard, his balls drawn up tightly as he resisted the urge just to plunge into her and claim her with hard strokes until he came roaring her name.

He schooled himself. Slow and gentle. He was no fool. He'd overridden her higher decision-making powers by seducing her while she was half asleep. She was a strong woman. She was possibly stronger than him.

He had one shot at this, one chance to get under her skin and make sure she was as addicted to him as he was with her. His balls hit her ass, and then he was in her all the way. He rolled his hips against hers, grinding against her and catching her clit between them. She whimpered. It was a sound he loved, so he did it again.

She was tightness, heat, and smooth silk all combined into one. His senses retracted from the world around him and expanded into a maelstrom of physical sensation. He felt every millimeter of his cock as he pulled out of her, then worked himself back in with short fast strokes. Each jerk caused a delicious friction that threatened to topple him over the edge but, he held on. He wouldn't let something as minor as his own needs stop him from pleasuring his woman until she was mindless and begging him for completion.

His hips set up a hard and steady pace, his cock sliding into her with an eagerness he hadn't felt since... well, since her.

Then it happened. Her body moved under his and his heart leaped as she began to respond. Her lips parted, her breath in pants. Around him, her pussy tightened in small flutters that threatened his tenuous control. He pushed her closer and closer to another climax. He wanted to feel her come all over his cock as he brought her pleasure.

Just the idea raised his blood pressure to boiling. A bead of sweat rolled down the center of his spine.

He pushed harder, faster, unable to stop himself. Grabbing her thigh, he pulled it up over his hip and drove back into her. Nothing mattered as his instincts took over. She was his, she'd always been his, and he didn't care who he had to fight to prove that, even her.

Triumph surged through him as she wrapped her

legs around his hips and hooked her ankles together in the small of his back. He grunted as electricity built at the base of his cock and expanded. A white-hot knot twisted and turned on itself, growing and growing until, with a roar, his body went rigid and the most intense orgasm he'd ever felt ripped through him.

CHAPTER 7

An insistent chirp drew Seth out of sleep. He snapped awake, his arms tightening around the sleeping woman on his chest. He felt his expression soften as he juggled her in his embrace and reached for his communications tag in the tangled mess of clothing on the floor. His fingers closed on the triangular tab of metal and dragged it free.

"Yeah. I'm here," he grunted. The only person who would call him would be his general, Jareth.

"Ah, good. Back in the land of the living now, are we?"

He threaded a hand through his hair and blinked sleep out of his eyes. "You know, we're really going to have to do something about your attitude. The way you speak to your Prince is deplorable."

"Yeah, yeah. Whatever." Jareth's voice was dismissive, the respect he showed in public replaced with an easy banter. "Listen, we've held off bothering you two love birds, but we just received a distress call from the base at Jenarlis Three, so we need to use the jump-field. We're going to lock onto you with a tractor and tow you with us as we head in."

"Go for it, we're done here anyway." He sat up with Jaida in his lap, feeling the slight lurch as Jareth locked the battle cruiser's tractor beam onto the shuttle.

She murmured sleepily and burrowed closer to him. He smiled and laid her down on the bunk as gently as he could. He brushed the strands of her hair from her brow. Her eyelashes fluttered in perfect half-moons on her cheeks as she sighed.

She was his. Even now he couldn't quite believe it. Far from the fight he'd been expecting last night she'd given herself to him so sweetly and trustingly it made his soul ache. That she was capable of that after how badly he'd treated her truly humbled him. And the sex... no, it hadn't been merely sex. He had made love to her, and he knew the difference.

Her skin had always been as pale as starlight, so

close to translucent he could see the throb of the veins under the skin in her neck. He frowned. There were dark circles under her eyes and she was too thin. She hadn't been eating right. Whether from the stress of being on the run or lack of funds, he didn't know. That killed him.

"Computer, schedule Lady Jaida into the med bay for a check-up and physical profiling." Dragging his clothes back on, he headed for the pilot's station in the cockpit.

He breathed in as he flicked his long hair back over his shoulders and started to braid it. The small cabin was filled with the heady scent of her perfume, and underneath it, a smell that was pure Jaida. That was what he'd missed. He'd bought a bottle of the perfume she wore, just to try and be close to her. It had never been right, though. The essential component, the bit that had been missing, was the woman herself.

He settled into the pilot's chair as they entered the jump field. It was a smooth transition, but he hadn't expected anything else, not with Jareth running the show on the *Vengeance*. The opalescence of the field surrounded them. Seth leaned his head back against the seat. All he wanted to do was crawl back into bed with her.

But he had a thousand and one things to do, especially if there was pirate activity around Jenarlis Three. The last thing the Princedom needed on one of the major trade routes was an attack that would cost lives and revenue. He sighed and sat up. His hands swift and efficient on the controls, he started the engines in preparation for dropping out of the warp field. The tractor beam could pull them in on automatic docking but it would be faster for him to fly them in. And time would be an important consideration if they had to go into combat immediately.

"This is the *Prince's Dream* to ISS *Vengeance*. We're prepped and ready for manual flight when we drop out of the jump-field. Release the beam three seconds after we drop out and open up the docking bay doors. I'll bring us in."

The comm crackled, a slight interference that would have let him know they were in a jump-field even if he hadn't already known, and then a cool, female voice answered. "Aye sir, approaching exit point in T minus thirty seconds. Ready to release tractor beam in T minus thirty-three. Vengeance out."

He looked over his shoulder at the slumbering form on the bed. She was still wrapped up as snug as a bug in the blanket. A small smile curved Seth's lips as a sense of peace washed over him. He had her back where she belonged; everything was going to be okay.

The shuttle lurched to the side. His attention momentarily off the controls, Seth was thrown sideways against the console. "What the *draanth*?"

He spun in his seat as the insistent squawk of an alarm shattered the tranquility of the small cabin. Then everything happened at once. One moment the view-screen was filled with the swirling opalescence of the jump field, the next they dropped out of the field and into real space. The Vengeance's tractor beam snapped off at the same time, leaving the two vessels side by side in the middle of a war zone.

Seth's breath caught in his chest at the sheer carnage spread out before them. Instead of the small but bustling trade outpost he was expecting, there was just destruction. The shell of the outpost hung against the panorama of the system beyond. It had been ripped open, the spiny struts of its habitat rings exposed to cold space like ribs stripped of their flesh. Most of the guts of the station were gone, scattered and floating around the surrounding area like just so much space junk. Except space junk didn't contain bodies.

Lots of bodies.

"Prince's Dream, this is Vengeance." Jareth's tone was clipped and no-nonsense. "Recommend you get your asses aboard this ship *now.*"

Before Seth could answer a raider rounded the bigger ship they were sheltering behind. Its ventral laser arrays fired in a continuous volley as it tried to rake a hole in the *Vengeance's* shield grid. Seth was familiar with the technique; Sector Seven used several variations. Take out one emitter, and there was a gap in the shield coverage. Keep hitting the same area, and that gap got bigger until it was big enough to allow a boarder to clamp on and cut through the hull.

"You aren't kidding Vengeance, you're crawling with vermin. Check your aft side and prep the bay for a hot landing." Seth's voice was just as calm as his second in command's had been a moment before. This—combat—was nothing new, but it was the first time he'd had Jaida with him. The first time he had everything to lose.

"Have that. You're good to go. Just make it quick, we can't keep these doors open all day for you."

"Sheesh, keep your hair on. I'm on it! Jaida... babe, get your pretty little backside up here and strapped in. *Now!*"

For once, miracle of miracles, she did as she was

told. Still wrapped in the blanket she slid into the copilot's seat. Seth spared her a glance as he gunned the engines and brought the small vessel around in a wide arc to get him on the right approach vector for the docking bay. For a moment he wondered whether the toga-wrapped blanket was a fashion statement, then memory kicked in. He'd trashed the suit she was wearing.

"Lady's mercy..."

Her eyes were wide as she looked out of the main view port at the carnage outside. The outpost was little more than a shell now. The wreckage of a base decorated by the slow blossom of explosions as the bulkheads within failed. Even now the pirates weren't done with the carcass, the bright red of scavenger vehicles moving through the floating debris and bodies to collect anything of value. With a sick feeling in his stomach, Seth realized that also meant organs as a medical reclamation unit started to gather the corpses in the distance.

"Sick bastards," he ground out.

The command console chirped again, warning Seth of an incoming sensor sweep. One of the raiders crawling over the *Vengeance* had pinged them, and as soon as it got back a confirmed signal, it peeled off from the larger ship in search of meatier prey.

Their grace period was up, just as Seth had known it would be. Now that the pirates knew they were here, it would a race to get aboard the *Vengeance*. Seth had seen what these guys could do. A split second too late and they would be overwhelmed, their small vessel ripped apart by the scavenger vessels.

"Hold onto your hat," he told her, his lips compressing into a grim line. "This may be a little bumpy."

He wasn't lying. His gaze scanned the scene ahead of them as he worked out how he was going to get them into the bay in one piece. As they watched, more and more of the scavengers lifted off the hull of the battle-ship and turned toward them.

Great. More company, just what they needed. With quick movements, Seth activated the weapons systems. The console lit up like a fireworks display. He fired off a quick volley to clear the left flank and gunned the engines. The air around them exploded as the *Vengeance* brought its lasers to bear as well, picking off scavengers as the *Prince's Dream* ran the gauntlet.

"Jareth you son of a bitch, I love your ugly butt."

Seth stretched himself to the limit to multitask. The Dream wasn't designed to be flown offensively by one pilot. They flew close to the Cruiser's hull, fast and low, hugging its sides. They flipped under the ventral side of the ship and then roared into clear space in a graceful arc.

The docking bay doors were a battlefield. Scavengers were piled three high as they fought the ship's point defense cannons to get into the docking bay. Already the word was spreading as several turned their noses toward them.

Seth's jaw tightened. How was he going to do this? He could fly the thing, weaving through the scavengers. They were quick and maneuverable, yes, but he was better and the *Prince's Dream* faster. Plus, if it came to it, it had good shields; he could ram his way through. Glancing impact he could handle, but if just one latched on with a thermo-lance, they would cut through the polarized hull like a hot knife through butter. The only other option was to fly slower, picking them off as he went, and hope to the Goddess he managed to get them into the shuttle bay before one of the scavengers broke through. If even one got aboard, then people would die.

Unacceptable.

He was running out of time. The longer he sat

here debating, the shorter his list of options got. Then the decision was taken from him.

Jaida reached out and activated the flight controls. "You fight, I'll fly."

Her expression determined, she took the flight computer offline and dumped the shuttle into full manual mode. Seth opened his mouth to argue, then remembered her piloting in the asteroid field. Jareth had been right; she was good, but with a reckless streak he knew from experience got people killed. That might be just what they needed right now.

His hands closed over the weapons controls and he nodded. "Hard left, try and come in on a low vector."

"Who's flying this thing pretty-boy, me or you?" She snapped. "You shut up and play with your guns."

"I'd rather play with something else," he threw back, a little surprised by the sharp quip. He'd thought she'd be pissed with him over the night before. It seemed not though. He smiled, his attention caught on a knot of scavengers trying to create a roadblock of sorts in front of them. "Roll for firing solution in three. Three. Two. One... roll!"

The shuttle rolled and fired in one slick movement. Triumph surged through him as the group exploded in front of them. The *Prince's Dream* cut through the wall of fire and debris with ease to emerge on the other side. He grinned. They worked well together.

"Yeah, I'm sure you would."

She didn't look at him, all her concentration on using the powerful engines and maneuvering the thrusters of the small ship to dodge and weave through the pirate vessels trying to lock onto them.

"Shit. These bastards really don't wanna give up, do they?"

"Nope."

He brought the *Dream's* canons to bear on the scavengers clustered around the shield generators at the edge of the docking bay. Damn things were like roaches. His fingers closed around the triggers and twin pulses of light lanced through the air, picking the smaller vessels off with lethal aim. "There. That enough of a clear run for you? I'd like to get aboard sometime today, if you don't mind."

"All over it like cheap lingerie on a porn star."

Seth blinked and just looked at her. He'd been spoken to that way before of course, but he certainly hadn't expected it from a gently-bred noblewoman.

"What? Don't tell me you never saw a porn holo before. If last night wasn't a lucky guess, I'm gonna have to explain the mechanics to you." She threw him an unrepentant grin, then gunned the engines and went for a split second gap in the battle raging around the Vengeance's docking bay.

His head slammed back against the padded headrest. This wasn't the woman he remembered. Hands firm and confident on the flight controls, her expression was one of cold determination. She could fly and fly well. He wondered what she'd done in the five years he'd been chasing her... not just driving a loader, that was for sure.

"Explain...? You want me to drag you back on that bunk and demonstrate?"

"Kinda busy at the moment handsome, gonna have to take a rain check."

The open maw of the docking bay loomed ahead. It seemed open to space, an enticing prize, but as Seth watched, light shimmered across the gap. His eyes widened as adrenaline slammed though his body with the force of a bullet. She was heading straight for a fully powered force field. If they slammed into that, no matter how good the *Dream's* shields were, they'd be flatter than a pancake.

"Come on, come on," he muttered as the bay doors got bigger and bigger in the shuttle's view screen. Jaida's voice was almost bored as she activated the comm.

"This is the *Prince's Dream*. Might wanna get that shield down unless you want a mess to clear up. Get the catchers and nets up too; I don't have time to slow down."

"You're nuts."

Seth grabbed hold of his seat. He'd seen some nutty pilots in his time, but even the most suicidal Sector pilot wouldn't be accelerating *into* a shuttle bay. "You're beautiful, but you're *draanthing* nuts."

"Yeah well, looks got me into this in the first place so forgive me if I don't take that as a compliment. Oh no you don't, sunshine." She scowled as she hauled on the controls and made the shuttle do a bizarre hop, skip and jump to avoid a tractor beam.

Seth couldn't help watching the force field with fascinated horror. They were so close, they couldn't see the bay doors anymore, just the shimmer of the field and beyond, the emergency teams assembled behind their blast shields, emergency teams who were waiting to pick them up off the deck plating.

The shield snapped off.

"Woohoo!"

Jaida whooped as the shuttle roared into the confined space. As soon as they cleared the doors, she slammed the brakes on. The straps of his harness cut deeply as momentum threw them forward. He didn't have time to wince or even think. Seth was reduced to mere reaction as the shuttle's landing gear hit the deck in a tortured squeal, rear port first, and they went into a spin.

Instead of panicking, she merely grunted and hauled the controls around to ride the spin out. They slowed, the view from the screen resolving from a chaotic kaleidoscope of colors into the interior of the bay. Finally, with a small bump they stopped, nose against the back safety net.

Relief shuddered down his sweat-slickened spine in waves as Seth leaned his head back against the seat. "You are totally crazy. Where'd you learn to do that?"

Jaida didn't look at him as they unbuckled, wrapping the blanket around herself more securely. "Outrunning Imperial troops on pirate routes. Death sentence if you get caught."

Surprise hit him again. "Knowing that, you're telling me?"

She shrugged as they reached the opening door, stepping through it with all the regal pride of a queen despite the fact she was naked under the blanket. "You won't kill me. You'd rather make me suffer."

Seth winced, the comment cutting him to the bone. After last night, did she really think that little of him? He knew she felt something for him; she wouldn't have slept with him otherwise. Although she'd done her best to escape him, and had transformed from the soft-hearted, bright young woman he remembered into something altogether harder, in that aspect he knew he was right on. Jaida would never be able to separate sex from emotion.

He uncurled himself from his seat and followed her. She'd given him her body, now he had to convince her to trust him with her heart.

CHAPTER 8

*J*aida walked away from the shuttle with her back ramrod straight and her nose in the air. The improvised toga swished against the floor, and the metal of the deck plating was cold against her bare feet. She stopped as black clad soldiers surrounded her and looked beyond her to Seth as he emerged from the shuttle. She risked a glance over her shoulder, and he caught her looking as he straightened up.

Her gaze wandered over his tall, broad-shouldered form. Even in unrelieved black with his hair braided into a single tail down his back his noble blood was obvious. Seth didn't need outward signs of rank or power. He never had.

"Okay, someone give me a sit-rep. What are we looking at?"

Instantly he was all business as he led the group out of the shuttle bay. Jaida walked at the back between two burly looking commandos as Seth fired off orders at the front.

She didn't know quite what had happened in the shuttle, other than being weak and letting him have her. She ignored the snide voice in her head. The sex had been amazing, more than amazing. He'd been dominant, demanding… and so tender at times her heart had wept. It had been everything she remembered and more. She shivered at the memory as they reached a junction.

"This way, my lady." Her guards started to bustle her in one direction as Seth headed the other.

"Wait!"

She'd already turned away, accepting that, in this situation, she'd been dismissed. With pirates banging on the door, she wouldn't expect any military commander to remember the existence of his bed warmer, at least until the battle was over, so the order took her by surprise.

The commandos parted as Seth strode through them. His silver eyes were molten, and the streaks in his hair almost glowed under the overhead lighting as he approached.

He stopped less than a pace away from her. Jaida tilted her head back and met him look for look. The swift intake of breath from all those around them reminded her again of her new station, little more than this man's sex slave. Seth raised his hand and silence fell.

A small frown creased his brow as he looked at her. He tilted his head, his expression confused for a second. She could almost read his thoughts as they raced through his quicksilver eyes. Confusion chased amusement. followed by deep, dark need as his gaze dipped down to the blanket tucked between her breasts.

He stepped forward half a pace, so close she could feel the heat of his body burning through the cloth that covered her body. He leaned down, his breath whispering against her ear.

"You have no idea how much I want to pull this…"

His finger drew a line inward along her collarbone and downward to the blanket tucked between her breasts. She bit her lip. He wasn't the only one who wanted to lose the fabric. As soon as he mentioned it, as soon as she heard the pent-up desire and raw need in his voice, it was all Jaida could think about.

In one swift move, he gathered her into his arms and took her lips in a searing kiss. Like a match to touch paper, need blazed through her body again.

She loved him. Lady help her, she'd never stopped loving him, despite what he'd done to her. Despite the fact he'd branded her a criminal and chased her across the galaxy, he was there under her skin. Like he'd always been there and she couldn't stop it, couldn't even ignore it any longer.

Her whimper was lost in his mouth as he pried her lips apart. His tongue slid deep to explore the soft, inner recesses within. Her breathing hitched, her stuttering in her chest. She needed this, needed him. She had for years, but she'd been too stubborn to admit it.

On impulse, she wrapped her arms around his neck and kissed him back. He stiffened in surprise, but then pulled her closer to slide his tongue against hers, teasing and tempting her as though they were in the privacy of his bedchamber rather than the middle of a crowded corridor.

When he lifted his head, her breathing was ragged. A small, very wicked smile curved his lips as he looked down at her. His eyes blazed with desire, just one look reducing her to a quivering mass. If he wasn't holding her up, she knew she'd melt into a puddle right there on the deck plating.

"Later," he promised in a soft voice. "Wear something nice and come to me."

* * *

"My lady, our orders were to keep you comfortable in here."

The guard on the harem chamber door sighed as he repeated himself for about the seventh time. Feet planted apart Jaida braced herself as another explosion rocked the ship. She sighed, wondering how the hell she was going to get out of here.

The courtesans had been ushered en-masse into the harem chamber because it was easier to guard them all together. The room was full of the sort of useless, pampered women who set her teeth on edge. To add to her private hell, most of them were in various stages of hysterics, so each new explosion brought fresh screams of terror and more fainting fits.

Initially she'd tried to help them, but any sympathetic feeling had long since worn off. They were playing up the drama to out-do each other, even though there was no one here to impress. If she were lucky, they'd knock themselves out as they hit the carpeted deck plating.

Although her wardrobe in Seth's suite contained all the same sort of finery the others wore she had dressed plainly in tunic and pants, with her feet in comfortable boots. At one time she would have been thrilled with the array on offer, but it just wasn't her anymore. Now she was more impressed with the sturdy boots and the quality of the plainer clothing. Stuff like this would last for years.

But she did stubborn well; it was a gift. Placing her hands on her hips she gave the guard her best mulish expression and went for the throat.

"How the hell can I be comfortable when there are people dying out there?"

As if to punctuate her point, the deck beneath their feet lurched again and somewhere beyond the open door, explosions and alarms sounded in a chaotic symphony. The guard paused, his attention fixed on the sounds coming from behind his shoulder. She didn't need to be psychic to see his concern; wherever those explosions were, then most likely his colleagues were as well.

"Do I look like one of these brainless bimbos?"

She gestured around the room, barely bothering to conceal her look of disgust.

The guard surprised her with a chuckle and a rueful smile as he rubbed the back of his neck. "I know. Why'd you think I'm stuck with this detail now? I was the guard you clobbered last time."

Jaida's eyes widened in surprise.

"*Oh, my lady.* I'm so, so sorry for that. Are you okay?" She bit her lip as guilt assailed her. She didn't like hurting people, even when there was no other option.

"Yeah. I'm fine. Takes more than a little knock like that to put a section trooper down for good." His tone was filled with pride, but then he seemed to remember he was talking to a woman who'd gotten the drop on him. He grinned sheepishly. "Only damage was to my pride, my lady."

"Please, call me Jaida. And you are… "

"Kel, ma'am… ugh. Sorry, Jaida. Kelis Travett."

She smiled and moved closer to the wall next to the door. She leaned one shoulder against it, her weight on one leg and her hands shoved in her pockets.

"Pleased to meet you, Kel. That's a nice name. How long have you been a trooper?" she asked, trying to get him to talk about himself. If she could just get him to open up then she might be able to find an in, something to help persuade him she could help. A girl learned to talk fast on the run; the sorts of places she'd been, her life depended on it.

He didn't get chance to answer. The ship went through its rock and roll act again, and more alarms joined the racket outside.

"Goddess, we're really getting a bloody pounding." Kel's hands tightened on his weapon, his knuckles stark white.

"Look, I'm a certified dock medic. I'm used to dealing with crush and penetration wounds in low and null-gravity." She tried her best to control the wheedling note in her voice. "Here I'm useless, but in the med bay one more medic, even one like me freeing up someone more qualified, might be the difference between life and death for one of your friends. Let me help. Please."

Kel didn't hesitate long. Another explosion, closer this time, rocked the ship and he cracked. "Shit. The boss is gonna have my *draanthing* hide for this."

Shaking his head at what he obviously considered his own stupidity, he backed up to the door and looked out. "Come on if you're coming, but don't blame me if this goes tits up. Now, look sick… okay?"

Nodding quickly she trotted after him before he could change his mind. The door closed soundlessly behind them. The guard on duty outside looked at them curiously.

"Problem Travett?"

Kel shook his head and motioned Jaida forward in front of him. "The lady just felt a little ill. Gonna take her down to the med bay and get her checked out."

"What? Now? The place'll be swamped. Can't it wait?"

Jaida stuck her nose so far up in the air that, had she been any taller, she'd have gotten frostbite. She leveled "the look" at him. "No, it cannot wait. Don't you know who I am? I'm Lady Jaida, the Prince's *favorite* courtesan. Since he has requested my presence tonight, I don't think he'd be very impressed if I was too unwell to attend him… " She let the sentence trail off and arched her eyebrow.

It had the desired effect. The other guard grunted and jerked his head in the direct of the medical bay. "Best get her down there then. Wouldn't want to be in your shoes though, Chief Med's not going to be happy having one of *them* in her med bay with wounded incoming."

She walked past him, Kel hot on her heels. It didn't take them long to get to the medical bay. The double doors were opened wide as people poured in. There were stretchers and wounded everywhere, the shouts of medics for supplies and groans of pain from the patients assaulting Jaida's ears.

"There. Bleeding's stopped. Just remember to keep the presser ramped up as you start in on those wounds. You'll be fine. Just work quick, okay?" A firm voice gave instructions from the other side of the room.

They both turned toward it. A small woman in medical scrubs stood on one side of the bed talking to one of the junior medical officers. For all his youth, she was smaller still, a child-woman with a mass of spiky red hair and small points to her ears.

Interesting coloring. Jaida suppressed the thought as the woman turned toward them. You never knew with other species which ones were telepathic. The name badge on the doctor's scrubs read "Dr. Sedj Idirianna, CMO." Clear aqua eyes skimmed over them in a two-second appraisal.

"Okay. You're not bleeding. No open wounds or burns. If you're not dying, I'm not interested. What do you want, Travett?" The tiny doctor marched over to them, her stride determined.

"Sit." She whipped out a small penlight and proceeded to shine it in his eyes, humming under her breath as she looked for a reaction. "You seem to be over your concussion."

"Charming as ever, Doctor. Actually it's not me I'm here for—"

She cut him off, her light gaze sliding to Jaida. "Don't tell me, the lady-bird here broke a fingernail. Sorry miss, you're gonna have to wait until I've patched all these troopers up. I think getting their guts back in the right place is a bit more important than your nail emergency."

Jaida chuckled and held her hands up. Her nails were short and workman-like. "Sorry, I don't do broken nails. Can I do anything to help?"

The doctor's expression was a picture of surprise. She was obviously not expecting that sort of response. "If you've got any kind of medical training I think I might kiss you."

Jaida couldn't help the smile as she nodded. "Low and null gravity medic certs, basic triage, and first aid. Hell, I'll even mop blood and vomit up off the floor if it frees up someone more qualified. Just point me where you need me."

"Hey… " Kel broke in. "If you two are gonna kiss, can you wait for me to get popcorn?"

The Doctor rolled her eyes at Jaida as she reached out and cuffed the trooper around the back of the head. "Pervert. Go do something useful like get"—she turned back to Jaida—"what did you say your name was?"

She didn't bother with her title. She was a courtesan now; she no longer had one. "Jaida."

"Go get Jaida a medical cover-up." She transferred her attention back to Jaida. "I'd like you on bed four over there so I can keep an eye on you at first. No offense but we don't usually get courtesans with any sort of medical training. *Any* sort of training, if I'm honest." The smaller woman snorted as she bustled Jaida over to the indicated bed. The medical officer working at it looked up then immediately went back to work, his hands moving swiftly as he applied burn gel to a vicious wound on his patient's leg.

"Helan, this is Jaida. She's going to cover bed four while you take a break. I'm assuming you can take over from here for him?" Dr. Idirianna's eyes were sharp as she watched Jaida slip the medical cover over her clothes and step up beside the tired looking medical officer.

"Yes. What depth of burn are we looking at? Have you activated the gel yet?" Jaida's voice was calm and professional. Bio-cool burn gel was often used on the docks. A lot of cargo was flammable and the sort of places she'd worked ran antiquated equipment. Being strapped into a loader when it went critical caused some nasty burns.

"Third layer. Gel not activated yet."

A man of few words Helan finished smoothing the violent pink gel over the soldier's leg. Tall and well-built, he wore the remainder of a Sector Seven uniform. He was panting, short fast breaths through lips with a bluish tinge. She reached out and placed a hand over his brow. His skin was clammy.

"He's going into shock."

Jaida turned toward the cart next to the bed and scanned it with an experienced eye. It was well stocked. Dimly she shoved her awe to the back of her mind as she picked up a med-patch and checked the label.

"What are you giving him?" Helan stepped away from the bed and cleaned his hands off with some disposable towels.

"50 cal of tri-direnalin."

She ripped open the small packet and slid the patch out. Careful not to touch the active surface with her fingers, she touched it to the soldier's neck and smoothed it down. "There you go, handsome. Soon have you feeling right as rain."

He managed a weak smile of thanks. She smiled, doing her best to radiate calm and confidence. She knew from long experience on the docks that a medic who flapped was no more use than a chocolate fire screen.

"Hmm. Good choice." Helan watched as she retrieved the small, pen-like activator for the gel to set it. He was testing her, making sure she knew what she was doing. Nerves assailed her for a second, but she forced them down. She knew what she was doing. People might see courtesans as pretty, useless ornaments, but she wasn't.

She set the device to eighty three percent and touched the tip to the gel layer. After a quick check to make sure there were no gaps in the coverage, she pushed the button on the side. Light built up around the tip buried in the pink gel. A small ball built rapidly, then when it reached the size of a pea, started to pulse. Waves of light rippled outwards. With each wave, the gel started to dry and turn opaque until it was a flexible and protective layer over the burn.

Helan grunted in approval. "Good. I'll leave you

to it for a while. I'm dying for a coffee. Yell if you need help." And with that, he was gone, leaving Jaida to handle the bed on her own.

It was hard work, but that was something she had never shirked from. She lost track of time and the number of patients the porters routed to her bed as the ship rocked and rolled around them. Each explosion brought fresh waves of casualties through the double doors at the front of the med bay. She was reloading her cart with medication and getting her bed cleaned down and ready for the next patient when everything stopped.

Silence settled over the medical bay as all the medics concentrated on the lack of noise from the ship around them. The explosions, the shouts, the distinctive *thud-clump* of the ships weapons being fired continuously… they were all gone and everything was deathly quiet.

"Is that it? Is it over?" The female medical officer on the next bed asked, her eyes wide as she listened for anything happening outside.

"Err… I think so, perhaps we won?" Jaida ventured. She hoped so; there had been far too many injuries and deaths already today.

As if on cue, the comm cracked and Seth's voice filled the room. "This is Kai Renza. We have defeated the enemy force, standing down to yellow alert. Good work people, we won."

Relief shivered through the bay like a tidal wave. Knowing they weren't going to be facing more waves of casualties, the medics leaned against their beds, exhaustion in every line of their bodies. Jaida snapped her gloves off and ran her hands through her hair. Her back hurt from standing for so long. It wasn't over though; there was still the clean up to do.

Turning she stopped as several of the newest patients in triage stood. Throwing off their tattered uniforms, they revealed bare chests covered with pirate clan tattoos. They were all armed.

"Oh, I think the Prince is counting his chickens before they're hatched." The voice sent shivers down her spine. "At the risk of sounding cliché, everyone down!"

CHAPTER 9

"Damage report. Put it on the main screen. Do we have casualty reports in yet?"

Seth barked orders left, right, and center as he prowled the command deck of the *Vengeance*. His uniform was torn and bloody. Pirates had managed to punch through the ventral shielding on deck fourteen while he was on his way to the bridge, which had resulted in a minor skirmish. The internal sensors had been tripped as soon as they cut through the hull, and by the time the boarding party poured through the small shaft, Seth and his team were waiting for them.

"Seven shield emitters out on the ventral hull, three on the port… they'd been about to break through, but the automated defenses picked them off."

Jareth, standing at the console behind Seth's command chair, reeled information off as it came in. His hands moved quickly on the touch sensitive console plate, occasionally reaching up to tap in mid-air on a display Seth couldn't see from this angle.

"Casualty reports not in yet. Odd…"

Seth shot a glance over his shoulder in surprise. "Not in? Is Idirianna on? That's not like her."

"No. It isn't."

Jareth's hands moved in a complicated dance on the display. Both men knew the diminutive doctor. She'd patched them up more times than they could recall. She was forceful, determined, and above all else, methodical. Not reporting casualty figures just wasn't like her.

Jareth looked up. Most people would have taken his expressionless face to mean he had no feelings one way or the other, but Seth knew him better. Even several feet away he could see the concern in the tall general's eyes.

"I'm not getting any response from med bay at all."

"Okay, check on the routing program for the

internal sensors. Computer, display main room in the medical bay on the main screen please." Seth flicked his dark hair back over his shoulders. It had come loose in the fight on deck fourteen. "Perhaps a power drain or something… " Jareth muttered as the computer thought about the query.

Seth shook his head. "No, can't be. Med bay gets priority after life-support and reactor containment. Their emergency generator should have kicked in when the power was cut."

Jareth opened his mouth to reply but the silky-smooth voice of the computer broke in over him.

"Unable to comply. No interior sensor feed for medical bay available."

"What? Reroute power and try again."

There was a short pause as they waited for the computer's response. All eyes were fixed on the main viewer at the front of the room, but it remained stubbornly blank, displaying only the imperial logo. Seth gritted his teeth.

"Unable to comply. No interior sensor feed for Medical bay available."

Seth turned and nodded at the two guards at the door. "Get a patrol down to the med bay. Move."

They didn't argue, didn't even nod, just turned on

their heels and disappeared through the door behind them. Seth turned back to Jareth.

"Initiate diagnostic procedures on med bay, then work outward until you get a sensor feed. I don't care if it's the camera down the hall, I want eyes on the place and fast."

"On it." Jareth's reply was short and sweet as he carried on working.

Seth resumed his pacing. Anger mounted and coiled tight in the center of his chest. Something was wrong. Somehow the pirates had found their way onto the ship, he could feel it in his bones. But how? They'd caught all the boarders and there were no other gaps in hull integrity. It just wasn't possible.

"Okay, got a feed. It's down two sectors but I can just re-angle this camera… Computer, put feed from sector seventeen, block C on screen please."

Seth turned as the screen flickered into life. The logo was replaced by a fuzzy image of the med bay doors. They were frosted glass with the medical caduceus, snakes coiling around a staff, etched into them.

As they watched, the doors slid open. A body was thrown out, tumbling to the floor in the middle of the corridor like a broken doll. Within seconds blood spread across the floor in an ever-increasing pool.

"Crap…"

Seth ignored the muttered curse from somewhere behind him. Instead his gaze locked onto the figure framed in the doorway. Tall and naked to the waist, he wasn't a member of Seth's crew. The tattoos that crawled up the left side of his body in a chaotic tangle marked him for what he was: a pirate.

"Zoom in on his face."

The camera zeroed in and the pirates face filled the screen. Heavily scarred his right eye was the milky-white of the blinded, offset by deep green on the other side. Heavy gold rings hung from his earlobe and punctured his eyebrow. He looked left and right down the corridor, then, as if he knew they were watching, he looked directly into the camera and sneered. He stepped back and the med bay doors slid shut.

"Zared." Seth's lip curled, his voice echoed by Jareth as both men recognized the face on screen.

Zared of the Yarin clan had been a major thorn in his side for years, more so than any other pirate. That wasn't surprising considering they'd had the same training. As a member of Sector Seven, he'd gone rogue on an undercover operation, married a pirate captain, and started a campaign of terror in the outlying colonies.

"Deck fourteen was a diversion; there must have been a secondary boarding party."

Jareth turned to one of the officers behind him. "I want a deck-by-deck sweep of the ship. Find out how they got aboard and shut down their escape route. Zared isn't here for nothing, and he'll have his bases covered."

He leaned down and picked up the laser rifle propped against his console. "And I'm going to take great pleasure in blowing them out from under his feet. Orders, Your Highness?" He cocked one eyebrow. "And if they're anything other than 'get down to the med bay and let's blow that *draanthic* away,' then with all due respect sir, you can stuff them where the sun don't shine."

A shocked silence rippled around the bridge. Seth felt the small muscle in the side of his jaw leap and pulse as he looked at Jareth's determined face.

"Do I have a choice in this one? Lead on, fearless one. Captain Denon, you have the bridge. We're going down to the med bay for some... vermin control. Raise the harem chamber for me and double check that the ladies are all okay."

An unbidden image of Jaida at the pilot's console

of his shuttle came to mind. Even a week ago, he'd have said she was exactly the same as the rest of the courtesans… a pampered airhead, given to hysterics and fainting fits at the drop of a hat. But after what he'd seen of her since…

The two warriors swept off the bridge side by side, a dramatic show of force, and Seth cocked his rifle just before they reached the door. Without a word, a squad of troopers in the black-on-black uniform of the sector peeled off from their positions and fell in behind them.

"Show off," Jareth muttered in an amused undertone as they headed down the corridor at a fast pace.

"Yeah. A little. Can't blame me, I don't get to do this much anymore. Too many bloody council meetings." Seth's lips quirked. "Any clue why Zared would do something so stupid?"

Jareth shrugged. "Stupid as in boarding an Imperial Prince's battle cruiser, or stupid as in getting himself shut in Sedj Idirianna's med bay? While she's in there?"

Seth's lips quirked. "You know, I almost feel sorry for him."

Sedj might be petite and cute as all hell, even if no one dared use the word within her hearing. Despite being a doctor, she was a fully paid-up member of the Sector, and rather a scary one in Seth's opinion. There was no one better at killing than someone who understood the way the body worked. He'd seen Sedj in battle a few times, and she was damn good at what she did.

"How about we just shut the door, clean the blood up later?"

"You are an evil man, Jareth Nikolai, you know that?" Seth chuckled as his comm. tag chirped at him. "This is Kai Renza, go ahead."

The voice on the other end was that of the bridge comm officer. "Your Highness, you wanted me to check the harem chamber?"

Jareth gave the order for double-time and Seth smoothly upped his pace as he answered. "Yes, everything okay? They're not too panicked, are they?"

There was a telling pause. Seth's heart flipped over in his chest. "What? Talk to me."

"Sorry sire. Yes, the women are fine."

Relief surged through him. He'd been half expecting to hear the pirates had gotten into the harem. "Except…"

"What? For the Goddess' sake, spit it out, woman!"

The small group stepped into the lift. Jareth

punched at the buttons to whisk them down two levels to the infirmary level.

"... the Lady Jaida, Sire. She's not in the harem chambers."

The world tilted on its axis. Gray pressed at the edges of Seth's vision as his fingers tightened on his rifle. His voice was tightly controlled as he answered. "Where is she?"

"The trooper on guard said she felt unwell during the attack, so one of the others took her down to the med bay. That was hours ago, and he says they didn't come back up."

Jaida was in the med bay. He just knew it. He *knew* wherever there was trouble, she'd be at the center of it. His heart threatened to freeze right there in his chest. He couldn't lose her. Not now, not ever. If she died…

"Okay. Thank you. Kai Renza out." He cut the comm and looked at the small group around him. They looked back, silent, their expressions determined. For the first time in a long time, Seth was where he belonged.

"Right, listen up because I'm only going to say this once. As soon as we leave this lift on the medical level, we are combat operational. The objective is to retake the med bay by any means, so I expect extreme violence from the whole bloody lot of you. As the man said, 'let's blow these *draanthic* away.'"

"Sir!"

The reply was echoed by all the men in the lift. With swift, practiced movements, they checked the weaponry they were carrying. Without really thinking about it, Seth checked the charge on his battery pack and grunted in approval. It was fully charged. A good thing, because he wasn't wearing a tactical rig so one battery was all he was going to get.

The lift clunked to a stop, Jareth with his finger on the hold button to stop the doors opening. "Okay. Heads up. Corridor in front of us hangs a left toward the med bay. The main doors are a hundred meters on the right. Doors were closed, they may not be now. There may also be guards posted. We'll work in two fire teams. You, you, and you on alpha team with me. You and you, you're bravo team with Princey here. Make sure he doesn't fall over his own feet."

"Cheers mate, love you too." Seth didn't get a chance to say anything else as Jareth released the button and the doors slid open. He lifted his rifle to his shoulder and nodded to indicate he was ready. On silent feet, the first fire team moved out, the four men darting down the corridor with Jareth in the lead. Halfway down they dropped into cover positions, making sure their firing arcs overlapped. Once they were all in place, Seth moved out.

His heart pounded, adrenalin surging through his veins at the prospect of battle as he headed past the first team one by one. Without looking back, he knew his own fire team was following him. His world was reduced to the view through his sights, the cross hairs overlaid on his vision as he passed Jareth.

There wasn't much cover in the corridor. The *Vengeance* was an imperial battle cruiser so the amount of clutter in main areas was minimal. For want of anything better, Seth tucked himself behind one of the support struts. Meager cover at best, but it was better than nothing. It shielded most of his body, and he planned to be firing back at anyone throwing laser bolts his way.

Bravo team poured past him, fanning out in the corridor and darting across the intersection to take positions either side of it. They'd be the fire-support as Jareth's team got a foothold into the corridor the med bay was on.

A small chirp from his tag alerted him of an incoming comm. The double bleep was the sector channel, which meant both fire teams were hearing it. "This is Bane. We're on the port corridor approaching med bay. I hear you guys have some trouble down there?"

"'Bout time you got your butt down here, Devil." Jareth dropped into cover next to Seth, his eyes sharp as he considered the corner. "Pirates have taken Medical, unknown hostiles, unknown hostages. At the least we know the medical staff—"

Bane cut him off, impatience in his voice. "Is the doc in there?"

Jareth sighed. "What is it with you lot and bloody women? I got prince-boy here mooning about, and now you're google-eyed over the doc... I should be running a *draanthing* dating service not a regiment. Tell you what, let me know when you plan to proposition the CMO and I'll book you a bed for when she hands you your ass on a plate."

"Hey!" Seth protested as he moved out again and passed Jareth. "I do *not* moon. Get your ass into gear, old man, otherwise you'll miss out on all the action."

He chuckled, catching Jareth's rude gesture out of the corner of his eye. The general ordered Bane's team into position on the opposite side of the med bay, organizing a dual offensive that would take Zared's forces inside by surprise. That was the plan anyway. All bets were off where the pirate was concerned.

The teams poured into the corridor, surrounding the glass doors. On a normal day there would be movement visible inside. Today there was nothing. Seth nodded toward the two troopers either side of the door. With the ease of long practice, they pulled spray canisters from their rigs and sprayed the contents over the glass. The liquid splattered then foamed up into a blue froth.

"Clear!" The one on the left announced as he slapped an ignition patch into the foam and turned his face away. To a man the group in the corridor followed suit.

Cra-a-ck.

The door exploded inwards in a shower of broken shards. Before they'd hit the ground Seth was on his feet with the rest of the team. Out of habit he looked toward Jareth who was leading the assault.

Jareth gave the signal to attack, and with adrenalin pouring through his veins, Seth led the charge through the door.

CHAPTER 10

"You all do exactly as you're told, and no one will get hurt. You have my word on that." The pirate leader and his men fanned out through the medical bay. Jaida was as stunned as the rest of the medics. How had they gotten aboard? Where were the men whose uniforms they had been wearing?

Her mind supplied the answer before she'd finished the thought, and sickness rose up from her gut, a hot wet tide that threatened to choke her. They were dead, they had to be. There was just too much blood for them to have survived whatever these men had done to them.

"Who's in charge here?"

One of the soldiers on a bed near her struggled to

sit up, the expression in his eyes angry as he looked at the pirates. "That would be me. Commander Benaris."

The tall pirate nodded. His mismatched eyes, one green and one white, contained no expression as he raised his pistol and shot Commander Benaris point blank, a single shot between the eyes. Benaris slumped back on the bed. His sightless eyes stared up at the ceiling as a trickle of blood ran down his shocked face.

The pirate looked around the room, arrogance in every line of his body. "I'll ask again, who's in charge here?"

Sedj moved. Not a step forward as such but enough of a movement for all eyes in the room to focus on her. Unlike the dead commander her face was blank as she looked at the pirate leader. "That would be you, obviously."

He clapped, pistol in one hand. "At last, someone with brains. Very good, my dear. And you would be?"

"The chief medical officer, Selena Norvairan."

Jaida blinked at the lie, her gaze dropping to the woman's white lab coat. The name tag that had been there earlier was gone. Confusion mounted within her. Why would Sedj lie about her name? As carefully as she could, Jaida scanned the faces of the people around her. No one seemed at all surprised by the CMO's lie. In fact, they'd all managed to remove their name tags unseen.

"Norvairan. You're not listed on the ship's manifest." Another of the pirates accused, approaching his leader's side and looking at a small data device in his hands.

"No, I won't be. I'm a new transfer. The old CMO bought it dirt-side on the ship's last mission, so I was drafted in to cover." Sedj folded her arms and gave him a deadpan expression. Her manner was the typical medical response of insubordinate with a hint of "I don't care."

Jaida had to admire Sedj's courage. Combat medics often end up fatalities on planet-side retrieval

"Fair enough. I'll buy that," he grunted. But the guy at his side didn't look convinced. Black, beady eyes glared at the petite doctor with malevolence. Two of the male medics moved to subtly flank Sedj. Out of the corner of her eye, she noticed another medic reach out and pocket a laser-scalpel while all eyes were on the CMO.

Jaida kept her eyes forward, not wanting to draw attention to the movement. Confusion and hope coiled in the pit of her stomach. A laser scalpel could be used as a weapon, which left only one conclusion. The medical staff planned to fight the pirates.

Why though? That was sheer suicide. The invaders were well armed and obviously knew what they were doing. But… why would Sedj conceal her name? Unless there was some reason she didn't want the pirate to know who she was. But why would that matter?

"Right, ladies and gents, I'm sure we're about to attract the attention of most of the troopers aboard ship, so if you could all make your way to the back of the room… Unfortunately I'm afraid your emergency exits today are… well, there are none."

The pirate chuckled at his own joke as he motioned them all backward. The others with him took that as the signal to move forward too, brandishing their own weapons.

"Okay people, let's do as the man says," Sedj ordered, her voice calm and firm over the subdued panic emanating from some of the medical staff. "Start moving the patients around to the intensive care recovery area. Anyone that can walk, walks. Beds for the rest. Here, you… come help me with this one."

Jaida looked around behind her then realized

Sedj was talking to her. "Oh right, yes. Sorry, ma'am."

Quickly she joined the other woman and started to unhook one of the medical beds from its computer hook up. As they were doing so, Sedj used her movements as cover to press a laser scalpel into the trooper's hand. His startled gaze shot to her face, but turned grim as he nodded, concealing the makeshift weapon in the covers by his thigh.

"Grab the corpse," the pirate leader ordered behind her. "We need to send a message that we've arrived."

Jaida started to wheel her bed toward the back of the bay. The skin between her shoulder blades itched. Each second took an eternity to pass, an eternity filled with the sound of her breathing and her blood rushing in her ears. Tension coiled tighter in her stomach as she waited for a shout from behind her. There was no way they were going to get away with this. The pirates were going to realize what the medical personnel were doing.

"Thank you, ma'am. Just turn me a little. Perfect. Now, get down behind the bed." The trooper on Jaida's bed used a large hand to push her down behind him. Crouching, she looked around. The medical beds that had been pushed to the back of the room had been arranged in an odd pattern. Almost random, but even her limited military knowledge told her the configuration would shelter as many people as possible... And provide a place to fight back from.

"Hey there, how you holding up?"

Almost on cue Sedj dropped down into a crouch next to Jaida. Her aqua eyes were large in her face but the expression in them wasn't panicked. It was clear and focused as she watched the pirates in the front of the room bundle Benaris' corpse out the front door. Jaida felt sick at their joviality and jokes as they manhandled the murdered man.

"Bastards. You'd think they'd have some respect."

She was reminded once again why she avoided dealing with pirates. Most of them were the kind of people who'd happily dance in their own mother's entrails.

"No respect, no morals. It's what they are." Sedj's voice was low as she answered. "Things are about to get hairy in here. What I need you to do is stay behind cover and not be a hero. Let us handle things. Okay?"

Jaida nodded and checked that the pirates still had their attention elsewhere. "What's going on?" She let her confusion show on her face. "You aren't reacting as I'd expect a doctor to. Doctors don't usually arm their patients during a hostage situation. Shouldn't you be trying to mediate… negotiate their surrender? Hurt none, that kind of thing?"

Sedj's snort was immediate and dismissive. "*Vaark* that. They came into *my* medical bay and killed *my* patient. They'll get what's coming to them."

Straightening her arm the doctor pulled back her cuff and showed Jaida the inside of her wrist. The ghost of a tattoo shimmered over the pale skin. At first glance it looked like the typical medical caduceus but, as she watched, the design shifted a little. Instead of the snakes being wrapped around a staff, they were wrapped around a winged dagger.

Her intake of breath was sharp as her gaze flew to Sedj's face. She'd seen that symbol before, on a report on Seth's desk. Right next to the elite forces logo and stamped "classified." The smaller woman was no ordinary doctor.

Jaida nodded once, the movement brisk and professional. Experience had taught her the best thing to do in a crisis was not to panic and find someone who knew what they were doing. Follow orders and ask questions later.

"Tell me what to do and I'll do it."

Sedj smiled and patted her arm. "Good girl, you'll

do well. Seth made a good choice... don't be too hard on him, eh? Any idiot can see he's head over heels for you. Why do you think he chased you for five years?" With that she was gone, moving on to the group huddled behind the next bed.

She watched Sedj for a long moment, shocked into silence. Seth loved her? How... when? She crouched behind the reassuring bulk of the medical bed as the thoughts chased each other around in her head. She'd always thought he'd chased her for revenge. Her world tilted on its axis. What if it hadn't been revenge? What if... her throat closed over as her heart leapt in her chest. What if it *had* been because he loved her and couldn't let her go?

She shook her head, not caring that people around her were giving her funny looks. They could think she was a stark raving lunatic for all she cared. She had more important things to think about now. Seth couldn't love her. If he did, why had he left a courtesan's robes for her after their first night together?

The memory of his valet holding the red silk out to her replayed over and over in her mind's eye like a holo on a loop. *Good enough to screw, but not good enough to wed.* The valet's exact words, or what she could remember of them. He'd been saying something else as she fled the room, but she hadn't heard it over the sound of her own sobs.

Cra-a-ck.

The sharp sound signaled the start of the attack as the glass doors at the front of the medical bay shattered and fell in a curtain of shards. Gas canisters rolled across the floor, billowing smoke, followed by troopers in black. The room filled in seconds with thick smoke and the sizzle-pop of laser bolts. She coughed, trying to keep the smoke out of her lungs as it burned her eyes.

"*Go, go, go!*"

Voices shouted above the noise of the firefight as she huddled behind the empty bed. The trooper in it was gone, his shadowy form sliding into the smoke, laser scalpel in one hand. She bit her lip. Tools meant to heal were now being used to kill.

"*Red, how many hostiles?*"

Jaida caught her breath. That was Seth's voice; she recognized it instantly. Everything in her, every instinct she had, wanted to leap up from the shelter of the bed and run to him. She bit her lip harder and forced herself to stay where she was. All she would do if she went to him was get in the way, and possibly get people killed.

"Red... you there, babe? Talk to me..."

Jealousy rose, hot and immediate. Who the hell was Red, and why was Seth calling her babe? She crept to the edge of the bed on her hands and knees and peered around it. The smoke was still thick, but she could make out indistinct figures just for a split second or so before they disappeared again.

"Yeah... I'm here. I counted eight." There was a bone-chilling scream, one that cut off with a sickening gurgle. *"Make that seven."*

Jaida's eyes widened as a female voice answered Seth. It was Sedj. So the doctor was Red... and from the way Seth spoke to her, the pair had history. Jaida swallowed hard, quashing the jealousy trying to rage through her system.

"Fire team one, flank right!"

"Cover me!"

"Hostile down!"

The shouts came from all angles as the battle raged. A laser bolt came out of nowhere and slammed into the bed next to her head. She flinched as red-hot pain sliced across her cheek, a cry of pain and fright escaping her before she could stop it.

"Hostile... draanthing hell, bastard shot me..."

The sound of laser fire and the following shout was just the other side of the bed. Jaida squeaked as a heavy weight slammed into it and made it rattle. Three more thuds shivered through the bed frame as someone, presumably one of Seth's men, slammed a pirate's wrist against the mattress to make him lose his grip on his pistol.

With each strike she tried to curl herself up into a ball under the bed. The pistol fell and clattered across the floor in front of her as above her, there was a choking gurgle. She listened with tears in her eyes as a man was choked to death above her.

"Thank vaark for that... hostile down."

Heart pounding in her ears, she broke cover, scuttling across the tiled floor on her hands and knees to grab the pistol. Cradling it to her chest, she dove back under the bed.

"Hostile down... "

"Hostiles down... "

"Bane... quit showing off. No way you got two!"

The shots were coming slower now as the troopers cleared the medical bay of the invading pirates. Everything went quiet. She tried to still her breathing, certain everyone could hear her. The silence was weighted as everyone listened for the slightest sound, the smallest scuffle, which could indicate any of the pirates left alive.

"Fire teams, sound off." The gruff command

sparked a series of names, Seth's amongst them, which presumably meant something to the asker.

"Medical, sound off."

Jaida crept out from under the bed, pistol held loosely in her hand at the sound of Sedj's voice. Straightening up she looked about. The smoke was clearing now, and it was easier to see. Troopers were moving around the fallen pirates, checking for life signs and in one corner sat the pirate leader, bleeding from several wounds but still alive.

"Someone get some cuffs on him and take him to the brig. I'll deal with him later," the tall man next to Seth ordered.

"He's bleeding, sir… "

"Unless he's bleeding out on the deck, I don't give a shit. Red, he likely to die on us?"

Sedj moved over to the pirate as he was hauled to his feet and his hands cuffed behind his back. He snarled and fought against his captors, but it made no difference. Quickly the doctor checked his wounds then shook her head.

"Flesh wounds only. He got off lightly. Get one of the civvy docs to treat him, because I'd just as soon put him down."

Jaida let the words wash over her as she concentrated on Seth. Dressed in a black combat suit stripped of all the trappings of his royalty, he was still magnificent. The black fabric clung to his broad-shouldered, heavily muscled frame. His black hair hung loose, the way she liked it, and flowed over his shoulders.

He turned and caught her eye. The smile that spread over his lips warmed her all the way to her toes. Hope blossomed in her heart as she recalled Sedj's words. Perhaps they could work through this... perhaps there was hope for the future. Didn't they say love conquered all and time healed anything? For the first time, she let her guard down and believed it could.

Movement registered from the corner of her eye as light from overhead glinted on a gun barrel. Fear wound its chill fingers around her spine as she turned. One of the pirates was on his side, pistol in hand and aimed at Seth.

Zzzzpht.

Jaida screamed as the bolt hit Seth in the side. He wasn't wearing armor. It sizzled across his clothes, spreading out in tiny bolts of lightning. His eyes rolled back in his head, a massive shudder racking his body as the charge hit his nervous system, doing who knew what damage as it arced through him.

She lifted the weapon in her hand. A second later,

the pirate was in the crosshair. She didn't feel anything as she pulled the trigger. A small red hole appeared between the pirate's brows. Blood oozed down his nose, and he slumped lifeless to the floor.

She dropped the gun and dashed to Seth's side. Tears cascaded down her cheeks as she dropped to her knees next him. His face was paler than normal, almost translucent and waxy. His eyes were closed, his lips blue. Blue lips were bad. Blue lips meant he wasn't getting enough oxygen.

A moan escaped her lips as the wall around her heart cracked right down the middle. She loved him so much, but he was going to die before she got the chance to tell him.

"Oh Goddess, no... please, no!"

CHAPTER 11

Four long, exhausting hours later, Jaida sat next to Seth's bed. Both her hands were wrapped around one of his as she desperately tried to fight back the tears. He was in recovery after a round of surgery during which she'd done nothing but pace up and down the corridor, wringing her hands.

What was with her? She *never* behaved that way. What would be would be, and the Goddess would decide the outcome of most situations. Even so, she'd prayed like she'd never prayed before.

Seth had to live.

He had to because, without him, her life had no meaning anymore.

Stroking her thumb over the back of his hand she

studied his face. Even in sleep he was gorgeous. A dark angel at rest. His skin wasn't so pale now; the color had started to come back when he'd come out of surgery, but it was still pale compared to the raven hair across the pillow. She reached out and smoothed nonexistent strands back from his brow.

"Well now, isn't this cute?"

Jaida tensed. The malicious, oily tones were familiar, ones she'd hoped she'd never hear again. Turning, she glanced to the door. There, framed in the doorway, was Seth's manservant, Warin. With just one look at his face, she was catapulted back five years...

He held out the red bundle in his hands, urging her to take it. "His Highness left these for me to give to you." His voice was level but the malevolence in his eyes took her back. She pulled the sheet tighter around herself. A heated flush raced over her skin at the thought of this man watching her while she slept. How long had he been in here?

She looked at the bundle in confusion. They were a whore's silks. Why was he giving her those? Horror filled her as her gaze shot back to Warin's face. No, it couldn't be. Seth loved her... he wouldn't... would he?

"No. We're going to—"

"Get married?" Warin's eyebrow climbed into his hair-

line. He chuckled. "Oh, grow up, my lady. You're good enough to screw but not to wed. No man buys the cake when he's eaten half. Take the silks. Let's be honest, it's the best offer you'll get."

Her heart shattered as tears welled up, hot and immediate, in her eyes. Seth had never intended to marry her...

She shook herself out of the memory and fixed Warin with a steely glare. Her hand hovered over the alarm button, but she had no cause to press it just yet. The instant she did, troopers would pile into the room. Then they'd want to know why and "because I think he's an ass" wasn't exactly a valid reason.

"What do you want?"

Her voice was cold enough to freeze deep-space tri-steel. She didn't care. She hated Warin with a passion, one that had only deepened over time. Sure, she knew he'd been following orders but the glee with which he had carried his duty out had created a deep and abiding hatred in her.

He'd been following Seth's orders... The same man who had chased her over the galaxy so that didn't make sense. What man chased a woman so hard if she was only good enough to screw? Time slowed to a crawl, then ground to a stop.

Jaida's heartbeat clanged like a bell in her ears.

The universe turned as, in one blinding moment of pure clarity, she realized the truth.

"He didn't give you those robes."

Seth came to by slow degrees, roused back to consciousness by the sound of voices in the room with him. The thing was... the conversation wasn't making much sense to him. It sounded like Jaida was arguing with... Warin? What was his manservant doing here?

Eyes still closed; Seth frowned. What robes? He had no clue what she was talking about, but the pain in her voice was enough to make his heart wrench. No woman should ever have that tone in her voice.

"Oh, give the girl a *draanthing* medal! Of course he didn't. Stupid cunt was obsessed with you, had been ranting on about getting married since the first time he saw you. Why do you think I had to get rid of you?"

Warin's voice wasn't the low, calming, subservient one Seth was used to. Instead it was bitter and filled with hatred. Why did Warin hate Jaida so much? As far as Seth knew, the two had barely met.

"He wouldn't look at me. Ever. Not once... and if he married you then I would have lost him for good."

Cogs clicked in Seth's brain, his body burning whatever they'd given him out of his system. Dimly he recalled Jaida screaming at him, pistol in hand, and then something slammed into his side before it all went blank. He'd been shot.

"He's mine and a little whore like you will never be good enough..."

Rage surged through Seth as he fought back to consciousness. Warin was a trusted servant, but no one called Jaida a whore. Ever.

"I'll have to kill you this time. To make sure."

The universe stopped. If Seth thought he was angry before it was nothing compared to the sheer fury that surged through his veins at Warin's threat. It started in the center of his chest, pumped around his body by his heart as it galvanized every cell. This bastard had threatened the life of the woman he loved.

Because he did love her. He'd always loved her. From the moment he'd seen her at her debutante ball, he'd been hooked.

She was nothing like any debutante he'd ever met. Within minutes of meeting her, he'd fallen for her. So, of course he'd done what every young male would do. He'd acted like a complete ass, driven her away, then spent the next five years paying for his idiocy. And to hear someone threaten her brought out a violence, and a depth of fury he'd never known he possessed.

He was going to rip Warin apart. Slowly. And he was going to enjoy every moment.

"You didn't intend for me to take the robes. You wanted to hurt me enough to make me run." The pain in Jaida's voice was heartbreaking.

Rather than give into the rage surging through him, Seth focused on freeing his fingers from the numbing lethargy. The tips of his fingers twitched and brushed slightly against the bedclothes. Triumph surged through him. That was it. Just a little more.

"I wanted you gone, by whatever means. When you ran, I told him you'd turned your pretty little nose up at his betrothal bracelet. Saying it wasn't good enough… He swallowed it hook, line and sinker. Must be used to spoiled little blue-blooded bitches. Another reason he's better off with me… I know how to take care of my men." Warin's voice was triumphant, lording his victory over Jaida, and his manipulation of Seth.

The fury in Seth's body turned arctic. He was an

idiot. For five years he'd been a *draanthing* idiot. He'd left his betrothal bracelet for Jaida but when Warin had told him she'd refused it, he hadn't even bloody *questioned* the man.

Move. Damn it, move!

Furiously he willed his fingers to move, demanding with every fiber of his being. Just a few inches further and he could trigger the emergency button. The instant that went off in his room, the place would be crammed with troopers.

Sweat pouring from him; he turned his head on the pillow and tried to get a bead on where Warin and Jaida were. The room swam and then started spinning like he'd been on an all-night bender. He blinked and forced himself to focus on the broad expanse of Warin's back. Towering over Jaida he resembled a giant. Even with her innate strength of character and the surprising skills she appeared to have developed during her time on the run, she didn't stand a chance against him.

The room whirled in a gut-churning dance. Seth gripped the bedclothes and squeezed his eyes shut.

"Nowhere left to run, bitch. Oh boy, I'm really gonna enjoy this."

Scuffles and the sound of choking filled the room. Gritting his teeth, Seth pushed the panic aside and locked it away. He visualized what he needed to do.

Open eyes, locate switch, grab, press. Simple.

Cold sweat rolled down his skin. It was Jaida's only chance. If he screwed this up, Warin would kill her. In his mind's eye, Seth watched helplessly as she struggled, her face going red as she scratched at Warin's hands. Petite and slender, she had no chance against her attacker. Her struggles started to weaken, the scuffling from the corner growing quieter.

Just hold on, beautiful. I'm coming; I promise I won't let him do this.

With all his strength he focused, bringing the seldom-used psychic power of his Imperial blood to bear, and forced the sedatives from his system. His breath hissed between his teeth as stinging cold ran down his skin in icy streams. The drugs Sedj had pumped into him oozed from his pores. Roaring, he sat up and slammed his hand down on the emergency button in an explosion of movement.

Cla-a-a-ng!

A metallic sound echoed around the room. Seth winced. Without the sedative muffling everything, his senses were hypersensitive, as if the world's volume had been turned way up. Twisting violently, Seth lurched off the bed, falling onto the floor in a tangle of limbs in his haste to get to Jaida and stop Warin from hurting her.

Pushing the hair out of his eyes, Seth looked up. Dread coiled in his chest as he expected to see Jaida slumped unconscious—or worse, dead—Warin standing over her body.

His lip curled back into a snarl. He was going to kill the bastard.

What he expected to see, and what he did see though, were completely the opposite.

Rather than Warin standing over Jaida, it was Jaida standing over Warin's unconscious form. The metal tray in her hands still quivered. Blood dripped from the corner of it as she looked down at the man at her feet.

She lifted her beautiful dark gaze to meet Seth's. His heart ached at the fear and panic in her eyes. Damn his weakness. He wanted to pull her into his arms and tell her it was all going to be okay.

"He's..."

Before Seth could say anything, the door was kicked open. Within seconds the room was filled with armed troopers. The red points of laser sights centered on Jaida as the only viable threat in the room. She squeaked and dropped the tray, throwing herself into Seth's arms. He rocked back as he caught her, his arms wrapping around her slender form as she buried her face into his neck. A mixture of tenderness and triumph filled him. She'd sought his embrace instinctively, turning to him for comfort when she needed it rather than running from him.

"Check that piece of shit."

Seth nodded toward the prone form of his former manservant as he pulled his love into his lap and cradled her close. She was shivering, and the warm wetness against his skin told him she was crying. He rubbed his hand across her back, the motion soothing as he rocked her gently. "If he's still breathing, get that wound dressed and take him to the brig. We'll be having a *chat* later."

He didn't bother to keep the bitterness out of his voice. His arms tightened reflexively around Jaida as he realized how close he'd come to losing her.

He'd pulled underhand tricks and cut off her access to any support network, thinking that if she had nowhere to run, she'd give in and turn to him. She hadn't. Under that alluring, feminine appearance, she had a backbone of steel. Rather than turn to him, she'd led him on a merry chase until Severnas Three.

A chase that could have been avoided if he'd stayed that morning and spoken to her himself. But no, he'd been too eager to prove himself to the council, sure he'd had that day's debate and his opponent nailed.

All the time he hadn't seen what a snake in the grass Warin was.

A small part of his mind tried to be rational and tell him that there was no way he could have known. Until today Seth had considered Warin to be a stalwart of his household, dependable, obedient, loyal. The kind of servant any noble would think themselves lucky to have around.

He snorted. Bitterness welled up and threatened to choke him. The trust he'd had in the man had been the reason he'd given him the most important duty he'd ever entrusted a servant with... to tell the woman he loved he wanted to marry her.

Idiot, idiot, idiot. What kind of man left someone else to tell a woman that? No, not just *a* woman. *His* woman

One of the troopers leaned over and pressed two fingers into Warin's throat. Then he nodded. "He's got a pulse. Okay, you and you, get him out of here. Get him checked out with medical then cart him off to a cell. Do not take your eyes off him; do not leave him alone. He's an Imperial prisoner and will be treated as such."

"Hear that, *kelarris?*" Seth brushed his lips against Jaida's brow as the troopers filed out. He ignored their curious looks. This was his and Jaida's business and no one else's. "He's gone. He can't hurt you anymore."

Shivers still racked her body. She refused to look, shaking her head when he tried to lift her chin. Seth suspected her eyes were squeezed closed. He pulled her chin up with gentle force. Reveling in the tender moment, he pressed a kiss onto each closed lid and then against the up-turned button of her nose.

Her lashes fluttered against her cheeks and then slowly rose. Her silver and sapphire eyes were dark with pain, worry, and something else. Seth blinked, unsure at the emotion he was seeing reflected.

"He's not dead, *kelarris*. It's okay, you didn't kill him."

Her lips compressed, anger flaring to replace the emotion he wasn't sure he'd seen and didn't want to name in case he was deluding himself.

"I didn't?" She shook her head. "Damn it, I wanted to. I wanted to knock his freaking head clean off!"

Amusement hit him hard and fast; that was his Jaida all over. Shivering with emotion one moment, and then ferocious as a tiger the next.

"I think you gave it a good shot. He'll be waking up with a headache, that's for sure." Seth tucked a strand of hair behind her ear. Already dark bruises were forming on her throat and her eyes were red with blood from burst vessels. He gritted his teeth. When he got down to the brig, Warin would get a damn sight worse than a headache.

"My little warrioress," he murmured, knowing his face was soft with emotion and not caring. "I'm so sorry, *kelarris*. For everything."

A frown graced her brow and she searched his eyes for a long moment. "Everything… everything? Or just everything?"

The forlorn note in her voice plucked at his heartstrings again. He'd wanted to give her the universe, but he'd ended up crushing her instead. "*Everything* everything."

Smoothing his hands down her arms, he pushed her away from him and stood. Sitting on a medical room floor was no place to have this conversation.

He knew what he had to do now. He'd chased her and she'd run, slipping through his fingers like a will-o'-the-wisp.

What was the old saying? If you loved something, let it go. If it returned to you, it was yours to keep…

He had to let her go.

"I love you, always have. Always will. Whatever Warin told you… it was a lie. I left my betrothal bracelet for you, not red silks."

She didn't move, didn't answer, and Seth's heart sank. Taking a ragged breath he turned away. It was too later. He'd lost her.

"I'm going to get a medic to come check you out," he said over his shoulder. "I'll arrange rooms for you aboard until we can get you back to your family."

He paused at the door, his head bowed as his heart cracked in his chest.

"For what it's worth, I really am sorry."

CHAPTER 12

Weariness pulled at Seth's body as he entered his chambers later that day. Contrary to popular belief, being a prince wasn't all wild parties, Herboriav champagne, and caviar. Mostly it was just plain hard work... at least it was for him.

Since the incident in the medical bay, he'd managed first to get himself released, which was not an easy task when your Chief Medical Officer was Sedj Idirianna. Arranging to have Jaida checked hadn't been a problem. As soon as the medical staff had heard what had happened, several of the doctors —all male, Seth noted with irritation—headed toward the room she'd been ushered into.

Ignoring the pile up and subsequent argument at the door, Seth had marshaled the troopers who had come to his aid, found some clothes because there was no way he was wandering around in a medical gown with his ass hanging out, and set about finding out why the last five years had happened.

Several hours later, most of them spent dealing with the particular brand of insanity that was his former manservant, Seth was ready to crack. Hearing the man's fantasizes and delusions, all built around signals from Seth himself, ones he didn't remember giving or that had been twisted to mean something else, had left him feeling sick.

He shucked his tunic off as soon as he got through the door. The rest of his clothes hit the deck as he headed through to the bathing room. Jaida. What was he going to do about her? Pain, love, and longing wrapped around his heart.

He loved her, but after what he'd done, there was no way he could ask for anything. Especially not after his recent conversation with her father. It had been perfectly polite and restrained. Duke Lianl had requested Seth return Jaida to her family and give them some privacy so they could tend to her after her ordeal.

In other words, "Give her back, and *draanth* the hell off."

Seth didn't blame him. He'd have done the same if he were in the duke's situation, especially now that the truth was out. Hell, if she'd been his daughter, he'd have hunted down anyone who had hurt her and had them hung, drawn, and bloody quartered.

All he could do was take her home and back off. Perhaps in time, she would reappear at court and he'd be able to see her, even if only from a distance. His heart protested, but Seth ignored it, stuffing the ache into a box deep inside and locking it. Maybe one day, she and her family would even let him apologize.

The door to the bathing chamber slid open. He stripped off his pants and pulled the band from his hair, shaking out the braid. The lights shouldn't be on. He went cold, stepping away from the door.

Water sloshed slightly, as though someone was moving in it. Seth's eyes narrowed; his attention focused on the small pool in the middle of the room. With the columns around it swathed in gauze, he couldn't get a clear look, but someone was in there. A very female someone if those curves were any indication.

Hope warred with excitement for a second. He could almost believe it was Jaida waiting for him in the water. Then the water swirled, and she moved out of sight behind one of the columns. His hope took a nose-dive. It couldn't be her... could it?

"I don't know who you are or what you want but you've got ten seconds to get that pretty little ass out of my bathwater before I call in the guard." He wrapped a towel around his waist and stepped into her line of sight.

He froze.

Jaida.

The water sheeted from her body as she stood, wrapping itself lovingly around every curve and hollow. Seth had never wanted to be water so much in his entire life. A droplet broke away and trailed around her nipple. Her sapphire and silver eyes were sultry as she raised an eyebrow.

"You want me to leave? Okay... if you're sure."

She started to turn and raised her foot to the first step. Seth was spellbound for a moment, watching the delectable curve of her ass as she moved.

"No! Don't go." He reached out as though to stop her, even though she was on the other side of the room.

She looked over her bare shoulder. Her hair

cascaded down her back in a mass of wet curls. Seth swallowed as the towel around his waist tented abruptly.

"Sorry, I didn't expect it to be you. N-not like that anyway."

Hell, I didn't expect you to come near me, period. If anything, the next time he saw her, he expected it to be when he was taking her home. Certainly not in his bath. Or naked. *He* looked at her in awe. Every inch of her body was locked into his memory after that night in the shuttle. But here she was, after everything he'd done, waiting for him.

If you love something, let it go. If it comes back to you, it's yours.

She'd come back.

The realization galvanized him into action.

Three steps later, he was in the pool, the water grabbing at the towel around his waist as he waded toward her. Less than two paces from her, he paused as indecision hit him. She hadn't moved, just stood on her step like the maiden goddess herself.

She wasn't a maiden though. She was *his*. Triumph and tenderness surged through him as he closed the gap between them. He caught her wrist, his touch gentle but firm.

"Please, don't go."

He pulled her toward him, the pressure on her wrist light enough that she could break away if she wanted. He was done being demanding and dominant. She came to him, stepping down and back into the water. Her eyes were dark, wary. All he wanted to do was take that look away and make it all better.

"Why?"

She tilted her head back and looked him in the eye. Somehow, even though she was as naked as the day she was born and physically no match for him, she was the one controlling this situation. This was it, his chance to explain and put everything right. Seth opened his mouth, ready to pour out the speech he'd been preparing all day, just in case.

Nothing came out.

Instead, he swept her up into his arms, claimed her lips in a torrent of passion he didn't know he was capable of. He opened her soft lips with a single sweep of his tongue, demanding an access she immediately granted. Groaning deep in his chest, he plunged his tongue into the warm sweetness of her mouth.

The kiss wasn't gentle. Instead he plundered, demanding her response as he pulled her closer, so close they seemed more like one being.

Desire and need swirled through him, making him lightheaded. His instincts roared at him to take her. His cock was as hard as an iron bar, balls drawn up tight to his body. Lady, he wanted to screw her... spread those pretty legs and drive his prick balls deep into her soft body.

No, not screw her. The very thought had him recoiling. His kiss gentled as he felt her fingers smoothing across his cheekbones and the soft brush of her tongue against his as she kissed him back. He wanted to love her and make love to her. For the rest of his life.

He broke the kiss and looked down into her eyes. "Why? Because I love you. Always have. And I'll go on loving you even if you walk out that door right now."

Water sloshed as he dropped to his knees in front of her. It swirled around his chest, wetting the trailing strands of his hair as he looked up.

"Jaida, you are my world... my stars... my entire universe, and I am so, so sorry." He shoved a shaking hand through his hair. He couldn't afford to get this wrong. "I'm a *draanthing* idiot... please, let me make it up to you?"

Her melodious chuckle filled the room, and

unbelievably she reached for him. Her hands were soft as she stroked the strands of hair off his face. Her tense expression was gone. Happiness and something else softened her face.

Seth held his breath in hope. Could it be love?

"I've always loved your hair." Her voice was soft as she tucked stray strands behind his ear. "You have more silver in it than before."

He nodded as she moved closer to him. Still on his knees in the warm water, he opened his arms. In a graceful movement, she pressed into his embrace. Something inside Seth's heart cracked and a warm, fuzzy feeling spread through his chest.

"You *are* an idiot. I'm glad you realize that." Her lips hovered a hairsbreadth from his. "But you're *my* idiot. And yes, I plan on making you pay. For years and years... until death do us part."

Seth blinked, hiding his surprise before he realized he didn't have to. Not with Jaida. He smiled slowly and stood, gathering her into his arms. He started to stride from the water, the only woman he'd ever loved in his arms.

"So... " she carried on, her arms looped around his shoulders as he mounted the steps and started to head toward his... *their* bedroom. Because there was no way she was sleeping apart from him. Ever again. "... where is it?"

"Where's what?"

"You owe me a proposal, dumb ass."

Seth laughed out loud as he pushed the curtains on the bed aside and laid her out across the satin sheets. Instantly he was by her side, stretching out beside her. His hand splayed over her soft stomach and slid up to flirt with the curve at the underside of her bust. Her eyelids fluttered downwards for a second, her breathing compromised. He smiled slyly.

"Oh... that. Well, I figure I need to add a little... persuasion to the mix." He leaned forward to tease her lips with his.

"Can't have you saying no, now can we?" He paused, realizing what he'd said. She'd said no before. "Oh shit, that wasn't a threat—"

Her fingertips on his lips cut him off. "Seth?"

"Hmm?"

"I love you. I always have. Now, shut up and make love to me."

Thank you so much for reading PURSUED BY THE IMPERIAL PRINCE! I hope you loved reading Jai and Seth's story as much as I loved writing them!

The next book in the IMPERIAL PRINCES series is GIVEN TO THE IMPERIAL GENERAL!!

Reviews help readers find new books! Please leave a review on your favorite book site! I appreciate your help in spreading the word!

ABOUT THE AUTHOR

Mina Carter is a *New York Times & USA Today* bestselling author of romance in many genres. She lives in the UK with her husband, daughter and a bossy cat.

Connect with Mina online at:
minacarter.com

facebook.com/minacarterauthor
instagram.com/minacarter77
bookbub.com/profile/mina-carter

Printed in Great Britain
by Amazon